Lyn

Enjoy the tattoo!

Laramie

Sass

A Stand-Alone Contemporary Romance

Laramie Briscoe

Edited by: Lindsay Gray Hopper
Cover Art by: Kari Ayasha, Cover to Cover Designs
Proofread by: Dawn Bourgeois
Beta Read by: Keyla Handley, Danielle Wentworth, and Carian Cole
Formatting: Paul Salvette, BB eBooks

Also by Laramie Briscoe

Dedication

Thank you to my amazing friend, Carian Cole, for being the person who gives me the hard love when I need it, and always believing in me when I don't believe in myself.

And to my grandfather, who I miss every day. I never expected that while writing this book, I would lose you, but I'm thankful for the 34 years I had you! <3

Blurb

I, Cassandra Straight, have loved Reed Shamrock to distraction since I was a teenager. I even watched him fall in love with someone else and almost get married.

A year ago, when he walked into his house and found his fiancée's face in his best friend's crotch, his life changed forever and it hasn't been the same since.

On his first night out since the horrible incident, we run into the ex-skank. Seeing the devastation in his eyes, I made a promise that I would help him get over her. I told him that a pretend relationship between us would work. It would help him move on.

I didn't count on my heart or his getting in the way. And I sure as hell didn't count on not being able to tell when pretend turned to reality. When it all implodes, the only thing left is the truth.

Sometimes though, the truth? It hides and we have to dig deep to find it. To make it come to the surface, we have to give it a little talking to. We have to give it a little Sass.

PROLOGUE

Reed

M Y WIPERS BEAT a rhythm against my windshield, clearing it of the rain that's coming down on this humid summer day. In the distance, lightening streaks across the sky, and thunder rumbles so loudly it reverberates in my chest. Turning on my headlights so that I can see against the greyness of the horizon, I run a hand through my wet hair. It's unusual for me to be done this early in the day, I want to call my fiancée and give her a heads up so she won't worry. I grab my phone and hit the speed dial then frown when her cell goes to voicemail, all the while keeping my eyes as focused on the road as I can.

"Lace, just lettin' you know we've closed up shop for the day. The construction site is completely flooded. I'm on my way home, babe. Love you."

Owning my own construction business, RS Construction, has meant a lot of late nights and a lot of long days. Even after getting it off the ground, there's a lot to tend to. The other day she made a joke that when we retire to the beaches of Gulf Shores, it'll be worth all the lonely nights she waited up for me to come home. But this afternoon, it can be like it used to be, before my company became one of the most requested in the state of Alabama.

I park in the gravel driveway—not yet blacktopped. I'm

working on it, but building the house before the wedding was my main focus. It was the most important construction project I'd ever done in my life. Building my home with my own two hands for the woman I love. Best. Feeling. Ever. I notice one of my best friends, Taylor, has parked down by the barn. There's a trio of us—Justin, Taylor and myself, best friends since high school. It's not out of the ordinary for any of us to be on the property at any given time. I have huge barns and storage buildings, and both of them borrow my stuff half the time. Today though, I find it odd with the weather we're having. Usually these conditions mean his body-shop is working overtime. I saw three wrecks in town before I hit the city limits. The hair on the back of my neck prickles, but I shake away the thought.

Turning the truck off, I put my hat on my head before sprinting across the muddy ruts in the yard—haven't been able to lay any sod yet either. Thumping up the back porch, I enter through the mudroom and unlace my boots to take them off so I don't track mud through the house. The floors are a nice mixture of carpet and hardwood, but the carpet is an off-white and wasn't cheap.

The kitchen smells amazing; my mouth waters and my stomach growls as the aroma of the BBQ Lacey makes for her catering business hits my senses. I realize how damn hungry I am, but I don't want to eat without her. We eat separately way too much. Plus, I'm not sure if this is BBQ meant for my consumption; I vaguely remember her saying something in passing about catering a wedding.

I don't hear her or Taylor as I walk through the house. There is no movement in the downstairs portion, so I assume she's upstairs. Maybe Taylor left his truck here before he had to take the wrecker out. It wouldn't be the first time he used my property to store his truck when he was out on a call. Taking the steps two at a time, I broach the landing and listen. Hopefully she's taking a nap, because I would love to join her. My dick jumps to attention at the thought. It's been a while, with both of us being busy.

"Lacey?" I open the door to our bedroom, but she's not there. The bathroom door is open, and I don't see her inside that room either.

A noise from one of the spare bedrooms catches my attention. We haven't done much in the room, so I'm surprised to hear noises coming from there. I slowly walk toward the door, not sure what's going on. Just as slowly, I turn the knob and enter cautiously.

My life as I know it explodes in a moment. My fiancée, the future mother of my children, is on her knees sucking the cock of one of my best friends. I want to puke, my stomach drops, and a rage that I've never felt before envelopes me. Pain, hurt, anger, disbelief; it's all there. How can two people who professed to love me so much, do this to me? Especially Taylor, who I've known since we were kids.

We've always been a trio. Justin, myself, and Taylor. Raising hell on the streets of Spartan County together. Smoking cigarettes and drinking beer, celebrating that we were All-State on the football team, giving each other advice on how to get girls into the backseat of Justin's truck we all shared. Crying at Justin's dad's funeral when we realized that not all of us are bulletproof and time isn't forever. Sitting on the back of that same truck, drinking our first beers at eighteen-years-old because death came knocking on our doorsteps one night. All those memories, all those happy times, all the bad ones too. They are gone in an instant. Our trio just turned into a duo. I'll never be able to forgive Taylor or Lacey for what I'm seeing right now.

A sound I don't recognize comes from my throat, and I yank her up off the floor before I land my fist in his fucking jaw, the other one at his nose. The crack sounds loudly in the room, and it feels good when the blood pours over my knuckles. He's bent over, cock hanging out, trying to staunch the flow. Looking behind me, I see she's against the wall, her tits moving up and down as she gasps for breath.

"Reed." Her voice sounds as breathless as her gasping.

I hold up my finger, fighting against the need to shove her into the wall and make her feel the pain I do. "Not one fucking word from either of you. Take your shit and get out of my house. If I come back and either one of you are still here, I'm cutting off his dick and shoving it up his ass, and I'll be shoving mine down your throat."

Those same stairs I took up two at a time, I take down two at a time, and I burst through the back door, trying to inhale air in my lungs. I don't know when I grabbed my keys, but I have on no shoes. Fuck it. I take the keys and splash my way over to my truck before starting it again. There's only one place I want to be, and that's with friends who give a shit about me. I look back at my house through the rearview and catch another glimpse of Taylor's truck.

In that moment the life I thought I had is over, and I know it will never be the same again.

Sass

I JUMP AS another jolt of lightening hits not too far from our office building. Again I curse my brother, Justin for not packing up and coming in before this storm hit. Over an hour ago I called him to let him know the storms were about to bear down on Spartan County, but he kept insisting they could get the job done.

Sometimes I think he forgets he's not the kid who had to make sure Mom and I had food on the table. Straight Edge is one of the premiere mowing and landscaping businesses in the tri-county area, not to mention the go-to here in our own county. He doesn't have to beg for jobs anymore, and nobody wants his fool-ass to get electrocuted cutting Mrs. Scotch's grass for God's sake.

"Justin, I'm gonna kill you," I mumble as I take another look at the radar on my computer screen. "If this storm doesn't first."

Headlights shine through the front windows of the office, but it's only one set, and I know that's not Justin. He had two dualies and a box truck when he left. Getting up from the desk, I quickly go to the door and hold it open, noticing immediately the truck is Reed's. He throws his body out of the driver's seat and slams the door, fighting against the wind whipping around the corner of our building.

"C'mon," I yell, even though my voice is swallowed up by the elements.

He comes running through the door, shaking the water from his hair. In the bathroom we have towels, and I know Justin keeps a couple changes of clothes—needing a change of clothes goes along with the business. Grabbing a towel, I throw it to Reed and lay the clothes on the desk. It's then I notice his feet, covered by socks. Normally, he's either wearing shoes or barefoot. As odd as it sounds, socks make me blush, because to me, they're intimate.

"Reed?" I'm cautious when I catch a glimpse of the look on his face. I've never seen the mask of devastation he's wearing; he has the look of a wild animal. It's almost as if he doesn't realize I'm talking to him. Beneath the devastation, there's a blank stare

I've never seen before. I approach him cautiously, putting my hand on his arm, talking to him softly. "Where are your shoes?"

He doesn't answer, and I wave my hand in front of his face. The lack of emotion and verbalization from him is starting to scare me. "Reed?" I question again.

He snaps his head up and looks me in my eyes. He's aged five years since I saw him yesterday. Pain is etched in the lines on his face, and the utter despair I can see makes me gasp. "What's going on? Is it Lacey?" It's the only logical explanation of what's causing this kind of reaction in him.

As much as I've always wanted to be the one to elicit this reaction, it's always been her. She's always been his kryptonite— ever since they got together, he's always done what she asked of him.

He's quiet for the longest time, and when he speaks, it's like the words are being ripped from his throat. He's clenching and unclenching his fists, holding them against his sides. "I walked into my house, and Taylor had his dick shoved down her throat."

I gasp, because I can't believe what I'm hearing. No matter how I've felt for Reed, no matter how much I've wondered over the years what it would be like to be with him, I never would have wished this on him. "Oh my God, Reed." I put my arms around him and hug him to me, hearing the pounding of his heart, feeling the anger radiate off of him. His arms don't go around me, and I realize he's fighting a battle within himself. He's trying to hold it together, but he shakes with the effort of it. He extricates himself form my arms, not ready for the comfort.

"Sass, I'm not sure it's a scene I'll ever forget. My best friend," he starts, the words cutting out as his voice grows hoarse. He stalks over to the wall and leans against it, letting the drywall take his weight, like he's too tired to hold himself up.

I shake my head, pushing my hair back so I can look him in the eye. "You don't have to explain to me." I want to save him this pain if I can; I wouldn't wish this on anyone.

He's pale and shaky, his breath coming in gasps. "No, I need to get this out. Why would Taylor do this to me? Why would Lacey do this to me? She was on her knees, on the floor with his hands in her hair, while he was fucking her face." He lets out a chuckle. "She never even let me go there with her."

It's then I notice his knuckles are cracked and there's caked blood on them. As he continues to clench and unclench his hands, new blood pushes past the cuts. "Did you hit her?" I ask, my eyebrows narrowing.

"What? Fuck no, I hit *him*."

I can't help the grin that covers my face. "Did you get a good shot in?" I walk over and pick up his hand, starting to clean off the blood with the towel he hasn't used yet.

"Think I broke the fucker's nose. Serves him right too." He licks his lips, pulling his lower one between his teeth. "I can't believe it..." He trails off. "I gave her *everything* she ever wanted; *anything* she asked for, she fucking got it. She was my life—I even footed the money to upstart that damn catering business. To be fucked over like this." He pulls away from me, pacing around the room. "Damn, this hurts."

I'm at a loss for words. I thought the two of them were happy. I thought they had a great relationship. Fuck, they were getting married. It was going to kill me, seeing him commit himself to another woman, but I was resigned to it. Just like I was resigned to living the rest of my life as a crazy cat lady.

"Reed, honey, I'm so sorry." I wrap my arms around him again. This time he lets me; he sinks against me and lets me hold him.

We've hugged throughout the years, and it's always been

platonic, because I would never mess with a relationship he already had. This time though, he clings to me, his strong arms wrapping around me and his head burying in my shoulder. I think for a sliver of a second I can feel his body shake, but then he pulls it together.

The door slams behind us, and we both jump as we see Justin. He's looking back and forth between us, barely leashed confusion on his face. "What the fuck is going on here?"

I can't help it, the giggles start, because my brother looks like a drowned rat. In between deep breaths and laughs, I get the words out, and Reed starts to laugh too. Between the two of us, we probably look like we've lost our minds, and Justin's stance says he's losing his patience. I pick up the slack for Reed.

"Your terrible trio with Taylor just went to a troubling duo."

Justin's brows pull together in confusion, and Reed clears his throat. "Instead of marrying me, I think Lacey's gonna be marrying him."

Realization hits Justin, and I immediately see anger back on his face. "That son of a bitch."

And like that, the Straight siblings have pulled in ranks with one of their most beloved friends. Justin and I glance at each other, and I know both of us will do anything to keep him from hurting again.

CHAPTER ONE

Reed

A Year Later

S MALL TOWN SATURDAY night in the South, and I'm doing
what I'm supposed to be. Hanging at Hank's Bar with Justin
and Sass. They've been constants in my life since my formative
years, and they've been nothing but supportive since the shit hit
the fan with Lacey and Taylor. My parents were workaholics,
and while maybe that's rubbed off on me, I hope I can always
keep these two close. Sass, in particular, is very protective and
never lets me get too far in my own head. If it wasn't for this
woman, my life would have imploded over the past twelve
months. She's done more than she's had to, and by the way she's
looking at me, I think that's going to continue.

"Do you want me to act like we're together?" Sass asks, her
mouth tilting up in a grin as she takes a pull off her bottle of
beer. "Ya know, make 'em jealous? Lacey won't be able to shut
her mouth if she thinks you've moved on to your best friend's
little sister."

She's commenting on the fact that Lacey and Taylor have
taken up residence a few tables down from us and are having a
grand old time showing me just how close the two of them are.
Walking in here with my arm empty was something I hadn't
wanted to do in front of her, but the fact of the matter is, I

haven't been out in the last year. I've been lying low, licking my wounds, and doing my best to get on with my life. The scenario Sass has presented is one that piques my interest.

I roll the idea around in my head. Could I do that? Would Sass do that? I'm not stupid; Sass has had a crush on me for years, but she's never acted on it, and neither have I. I glance over at Lacey, noticing she's looking at me too. There's interest in her eyes, and a little bit of jealousy as she sees Sass lean closer. Oh fuck yeah, this will work. We'll make it work, crushes be damned. I've moved on from hurt—I'm to the point in my grieving process where I want to dish out some good old-fashioned pay back.

"C'mon." I tilt my head at her as I pull back my chair and pat my thigh. "Let's do this." I look over and wink at Justin, hoping he realizes I'm playing—that this isn't what it looks like to people on the outside looking in. There's not a smile on his face, or a look of understanding, I'm going to have some explaining to do. Since this will never go anywhere, that's not a problem, and it's a concession I'm willing to make.

There's a mischievous grin on Sass's face, and I know without a doubt she's going to put her all into this. Sass does nothing half-assed; never has and never will. She shakes her ass as she walks towards me, situating herself on my leg so we're in prime view of Lacey and Taylor. She sits there, pressing herself into my side as I lazily swing my arm around her back, cupping her hip, letting my hand linger on her butt cheek. "She's looking over here," Sass whispers as she puts her mouth to my ear.

I cut my eyes over to where I know Lacey is, and for a moment the two of us catch each other's glances. There's a pain on her face I hadn't expected, red color riding high on her cheeks. Jealousy. I recognize it well, because I've seen it many times over the years. I let a smile spread across my face, because knowing that she's jealous feels fucking good.

"Good, I hope she realizes what the fuck she's missing. Bitch could have been marrying me tomorrow."

The words are said in a joking manner, but I mean them. Our wedding date was scheduled for the next day—before she decided to stab me in the back and fuck one of my closest friends. I pull Sass closer, push my hand up around the small of her back and let my fingers play against the soft skin. It was one of the things Lacey used to love for me to do. I make sure our eyes meet again and offer her a smart-ass wink. I hope the show I'm putting on makes her believe I'm better off since she left.

But I'm not. I've been pretty fucking miserable. Tonight is my first night delving back into the nightlife of small-town Alabama, and I sure as fuck didn't think I'd see her here.

Sass pulls me into her as she bends down. "Go with it." Her lips smash into mine, her fingers tangle in my hair and tug, and regardless of how this started—my body reacts. I can't even be embarrassed because I know Lacey sees it. I hope she knows she doesn't have me by the dick anymore, and I hope she and Taylor Carter are fucking happy together, because starting now, I'm taking back my life. I feel her eyes on me as I break the kiss with the woman I'm holding in my arms. I'm shaky and not sure what just happened between the two of us, but right now, all I know is it hurt the woman who would have been my wife. I can see it in her eyes as she strolls over to our table.

"Can we help you?" I ask, my eyebrows up in my hairline. I try to affect a bored look, but right now I'm hard as a rock and trying desperately not to make Sass uncomfortable.

"Didn't know you were slumming with Justin's kid sister." Lacey sneered, showing me in two seconds flat the kind of person I would have married.

I smile patiently at her, running my tongue over the lips Sass has just thoroughly kissed. I can taste the coconut flavor of her lip gloss, and it's a welcome distraction from the taste of bitterness I've been trying to get rid of for the past year. It gives me hope that maybe I can overcome this.

"Slumming? Really? At least I don't take my best friend's sloppy seconds, and her lips taste better than yours ever did."

She's speechless as she looks at me. For so long I haven't had a backbone when it came to the hurt she'd placed in my heart. I have it now, and fuck it; I'm doing whatever it takes to keep it.

"So you're a thing?" she asks, her lip curled.

Her eyes go back and forth between us. They land on Sass, and I can see it; she's eyeing her up and down like she's competition. This time, though, there is no competition. Lacey had me once, and she threw it away; I'm not stupid enough to put myself back in that situation any longer. I may be a lot of things, but a glutton for punishment is not one of them.

"We are." I caress the ass sitting in my lap as my eyes meet Lacey's. I make sure she sees it, and again I see a ribbon of jealousy in her eyes. I make a decision. I'm all in, because this is revenge I want, something I want to throw back in her face if given the chance. I want to; I want to be a man someone wants, not the man someone can throw to the wayside when they're done. That shit hurts like a motherfucker, and I'm sick of hurting.

The little white lie will never hurt anyone. We'll play the game and we'll win. Reed Shamrock is done being the man who got his entire world rocked when he found his fiancée on her knees sucking his best friend's cock.

For the first time in months, I feel like I'm in control.

CHAPTER TWO

Sass

I EYE LACEY as she walks away from us, resting myself against Reed's side like I belong there. Because really, there's nothing I won't do for him, and it's been that way since I was a teenager.

Being a fourteen-year-old who's growing into herself isn't exactly the best place to be in life. I'm gangly. My legs are too long, my chest is too small, and the braces that are supposedly going to make my teeth straight don't do anything for my smile right now. It makes me more self-conscious, and I hate it. Walking over to the full-length mirror in my bedroom, I take a look at myself, wondering when I'll be beautiful. I wonder when I'll be the girl who catches the eye of the guys. Of one guy in particular. My brother's best friend, Reed Shamrock.

He's everything I think a boyfriend should be. He's nice to me, doesn't make fun of me, and he smiles easily. I hardly ever see my older brother, Justin, smile. At least not anymore. Reed though? He always has a smile for me, a little joke, or a question to ask. Not to mention he's got muscles on top of muscles. Lately he's been sporting a little bit of scruff, and his hair is longer than he's ever had it. It touches the edges of his shirt—whenever he wears one.

Reed's kinda my hero. Less than a year ago, when my dad died, he found me crying on the roof of our house. He sat with me for hours as we talked about our favorite memories, and then he hugged me against his chest when we lapsed into complete silence. He never once pressured me to keep talking, never once made me think I was stupid for crying, and he never tried to make light of the subject. I'll never, ever forget that, and I don't think he knows, even now, how much it meant to me.

"Sass, you here?"

It's Justin, probably checking to make sure I've made it home from school okay. I'm fourteen, but you would think I'm six. He likes to check in, every single day, to make sure I'm not off doing illegal things I'm not supposed to be doing. I roll my eyes, thankful he can't see me. He's lectured me about being responsible a lot lately.

"Be right down." I purposely yell louder than I need to. Hopefully he gets the message that I don't need him checking up on me every day.

As I get to the bottom of the stairs, I'm greeted not only by my brother but by Reed as well. My face immediately flames because of the thoughts I was having not too long ago. Judging by the way they look, they've obviously been out cutting yards. It's what my brother does now that he's graduated high school. Reed has been working with a friend with a construction business, but when he finishes a job or construction is slow, he tries to help Justin knock out a few yard jobs. I heard them talking the other day, and Justin admitted the money he makes from cutting yards is the only thing keeping my family afloat financially, and it makes me look up to Reed even more. Deep in my heart, I know this hero worship will one day be the death of me.

My eyes can't help but take in Reed's strong profile. I hope he doesn't realize how powerful this crush I have on him is. I hope it's not obvious in my eyes how much I think constantly about how he hugged me on the rooftop. How I wanted it to be so much more than the way a brother hugs a sister; I wanted it to be the way a guy hugs a girl he likes.

"You get home okay?" Justin asks as he hurries into the kitchen. He goes around the small space, grabbing stuff to make him and Reed some sandwiches.

The room is quiet as both of them down bottles of water in record time. "Yeah, I didn't have a problem with the new bus route." I try not to let my voice sound thin. After dad died, our mom couldn't afford the house they'd lived in since they had gotten married. Now we live in a cheaper house, further out in the county. It's been a hard adjustment. I had both my home and my dad taken away from me in the span of months.

Justin ruffles my hair. "You'll be drivin' before long anyway, and if Reed or I can get away, we'll come get you when we can."

It's a promise I've heard many times before. One I know he'll keep, but it doesn't make this situation any easier.

"It's okay." I smile up at both of them, my eyes not meeting Reed's completely. "We do what we gotta do. I understand."

Justin takes another bite of his sandwich. "I appreciate you doing everything Mom and I have asked you to do, Sass. You're helping us by doing what you're supposed to do and keeping yourself out of trouble."

I nod, but I can't say anything because of the lump in my throat. Some days it feels like it's never going to go away, other days it's not so hard to swallow around. Today is one of the difficult days.

I wait for him to speak again, but he grabs his sandwich, taking it to the living room as he mumbles about calling his girlfriend, Morgan.

"It's still just as hard for him as it is for you," Reed confesses softly as he leans in and puts his arm around my shoulder. "He doesn't know how to make things easier for any of you, and it's tearing him up, so be sure and give him a break. He's doing the best he can, and he's got a lot on his plate right now. You keep doing what you're doing."

"I will." At this moment, some sort of dam breaks inside me, and embarrassing tears spill forth. I fight to get my breath while trying to unlock the tightness in my chest. I can't believe I'm crying—again—in front of the guy I have the biggest crush on.

I try to turn away, but he doesn't let me. Instead, he uses his arms to pull me into a hug. I collapse against him, not realizing how much I need someone to hold me up, sobbing like I haven't allowed myself to do since my dad died. Like I haven't been able to do in front of my mom and brother.

In this moment, as Reed Shamrock lets me cry against him, I, Cassandra Straight, fall head over heels in love; damn the six-year age difference. As he lets me grieve in his arms, I know when we get older he will want no one but me. He will be mine, and I'll be his. It's a clarity I've never had before.

Bless my crazy little fourteen-year-old heart.

CHAPTER THREE

Sass

THE SCENE FROM last night plays over and over in my head, like the highlight reel of a football game. The culmination of my entire teenage dreams of love and marriage are wrapped up in the man I'm now calling mine. I can't believe Reed and I told his ex-fiancée we're a couple. It'll be all over town soon, and we won't be able to escape it, but I'm okay with that. I've had a thing for Reed for as long as I can remember, and if this is a way for me to get into his life, then I'll take it as the gift it is. I'll put myself out there, and maybe when the time comes, he won't be able to let me leave.

I'm working on invoicing for the family business when my brother comes pounding up the front steps, throwing the door open.

"You've lost your damn mind." He shakes his head as he plops down in the chair in front of the desk.

Last night we all drove ourselves to the bar, and I didn't have to listen to the lecture I think is about to come. From the grim set of his mouth, and the way his eyes keep darting back and forth, he's been working up a good one all day.

"How's that?" I ask, but I know the answer. This is all about Reed.

"You're playing with fire, baby girl." He shakes his head

again, using the nickname our dad used for me. "Do you honestly think you can pretend to be in a relationship with Reed and not end up gutted when it's over? Where is your fuckin' head?"

I'm used to him being pissed off, used to him questioning most of what I do, but to be honest, I hadn't been sure he would question my motives with Reed, or his motives with me. I thought we were pretty damn transparent, for the most part.

"My head is in wanting to help Reed. You and I have both seen how lonely he's been this year, how much of a shell he's been of the former person we knew. He needed help, and this is help I can give him," I defend myself. "Besides, Justin, it's not real. I know and I understand that."

He scoots forward in his chair and levels me with a stare. "Do you really, Sass? Do you understand as the two of you pretend, you're going to come to a point where you aren't going to know what's real and what's not? You've wanted this for so fucking long, you're not going to know, I don't care what you say. You're not going to know."

I shoot him what I hope is a bored look. Trying to explain this to him isn't going the way I want it to. He's not giving me room, and he's not letting me be the adult I am. He's never been very flexible where I'm concerned, especially since our dad died, always seeing himself as the man of the house and my protector. "You saw his face last night when he saw her, and you saw her face when she saw the two of us together. This is going to do exactly what he wants it to do, and maybe in the end, I'll get him out of my system. Either way, people hopefully won't refer to him as the guy who got fucked over by his best friend." I shrug as I continue entering data, like it's not a big deal.

"So you're letting him use you?" His voice is hard, disbeliev-ing. Like he can't believe I'm letting this happen, but how can I not? Even if it's not completely true, it's what I've always wanted.

I try to make him understand. "I'm using him too. Can you imagine what a catch I'll be in this town after Reed Shamrock dumps me?" I ask, silently praying it won't happen.

Justin turns to look at me, really look at me. He can see through me most of the time, and I hate it. There are things I like to keep hidden, things I don't want him to see, I don't want him to know. He does, though, every time. "Sass, you may think I don't know what's going on in your life, or your head, but I'm not stupid. Don't set yourself up for a heartbreak like this unless you can take it. Reed doesn't need you to save him."

"That's not what I'm trying to do at all," I argue—even though I *am* trying to save him. I don't want him to hurt for her anymore. I want him to live for me. "I'm helping a friend. That's all this is. Don't look any deeper in it than you need to."

He looks like he wants to say more. "I could tell you the same thing, but you're a grown woman, and you're gonna do what you want to do. Just be careful, that's all I ask."

I love him for doing this, I love him for being my big brother, but I can make my own life decisions—whether they be good or bad. "I will. I promise."

He gets up and puts his hat on. "The only other thing I ask is you don't force me to choose. He's been my best friend since we were kids. I don't want to have to make a decision. You will always come first, but he's as much my family as you are. And face the fact I'm gonna have to kick his ass for even agreeing to this stupid stunt. It might not come today, it might not come tomorrow, but he's gonna get an ass whoopin' from me."

"I would never make you do that, Justin. If things go south with this, then I promise it won't affect your relationship with either one of us." I mean what I've said, but even I know life sometimes happens, and none of us can prevent it.

He leans in, giving me a hug. "I'm gonna hold you to that."

He leaves the office, and I hope like hell I haven't lied my ass off to him. Against everything I should hope for, I hope maybe this game we're playing may turn real, and maybe, just maybe, I won't get my heart broken.

Reed

SOUTHERN ALABAMA IS fucking hot in the summer time. Today is no exception. Working in construction in this heat is miserable, and I like to make sure my guys are well taken care of. The last thing I need is for any of them to have heat stroke, me included.

"Let's take a break." I pull my shirt up and run it along my forehead.

They all head towards the canopy I've set up, getting water out of the iced coolers I keep there. I found out early on with my business, if I take care of my crew, they take care of me. I hang back until the end, letting them go first.

When it's my turn, I grab a bottle of water, twist the cap off, and tip my head back. I let the cold water run down my parched throat, trying not to gulp so much it'll cause me to be sick. Out of the corner of my eye, I spot a large truck rolling up to our construction site and notice Straight Edge's logo on the side. The door opens, and a long, tan leg reaches down from inside, putting a sneaker-covered foot on the running board.

"Hot damn," one of my guys says. "I'd like to get a piece of that."

I smack him in the head, jealousy roaring up unexpectedly in my stomach. "That's Justin's sister, dude, and she and I are kind of dating at the moment. Keep your mouth shut."

"My bad." He puts his hands up in surrender. "I didn't know."

"It's new." My voice is agitated as she finishes getting out of the truck and pulls her sunglasses up over her head. "Get back to work," I bark out the order as I walk over to meet her.

"Hey." She smiles at me, reaching up to give me a hug and a kiss on the cheek.

She's always done this when she greets me; I don't know why it feels different this time. "Hey, yourself. Not that I don't like seeing you, but your brother should be here today, not you."

"I know." She walks back to the truck, hopping up onto the running board, and reaching in to grab an iPad mini. The way she bows her body and stretches makes her cut-offs pull tight against her ass, rising so far I can see the beginning swell of a cheek. *Holy fucking shit.* She's still talking and I do my best to pay attention. "One of the crews got too close to a pond and got stuck. He's helping them get situated and sent me out on this and the next project so we could keep things moving. He's pissed as all hell."

"He's an ass, considering how hot it is out here," I said, nodding at the worn cut-offs and her tank top.

"I'm wearing as little as I can while still being decent. I hope it's enough." She laughs.

"My crew definitely noticed." I hope she takes that into account if she ever wants to come see me again. Hopefully she'll wear more clothing.

She wrinkles her nose in a cute way, tilting her head up towards me. "The question I want to ask Reed Shamrock is, did you notice?"

I can't even lie, and maybe it makes me a bastard, because I'm not supposed to be noticing. She's not really mine to notice, but I can't make her think I don't appreciate how good she looks either. "I did. Couldn't help but notice."

The twinkle in her eye tells me I'm in big trouble, but at this point, I'm not sure I care.

CHAPTER FOUR

Sass

REED IS RIGHT, it is hot out here, too hot to be legal. I hold up the hair at the back of my neckline, hoping to give the skin some breathing room. Even though I have it in a ponytail, it's still sticking, piece by piece, to the sweat that's gathered on my skin. We're measuring for the sod Reed's customer wants to lay in the backyard, and I'm having a hard time concentrating. Some of it is the heat, but the other part of it is him.

I've seen Reed on construction sites a lot over the past few years, especially as I've started to help Justin out more, finally becoming full-time for him earlier this year. It's never hit me quite like this before. Pulling up in the company truck, I saw him, and it was almost as if I'd never seen him before—at least not like this. Reed's always been a good looking guy, but today he is a hot-as-fuck man.

I shiver, even though I'm burning up, as I remember the first glance I had of him. Faded, dirty jeans, a rip in his right knee. Boots covering his feet; although they've seen better days, there's something about them being so lived-in that makes my mouth water. His shirt, oh my God, his shirt. It's white, and the sweat has caused it to stick against his abs; I can see them every time he moves. His abs—I could write poetry about, and possibly sacrifice body parts for. There's also this little streak of dirt across his cheek, and even the streak of dirt makes my lady parts quiver. He looks like a *man*, and I don't think in all of my twenty-four years have I ever really had a man. I pray to every God I know I'll find out what this particular man is like.

"Alright, that's it." He pulls up the measuring device we're using. "You mind if we do the front yard real fast? The owners were here yesterday and mentioned if sod prices came down, they would be willing to do the front yard too. I wanna get 'em an estimate no matter what. It might be cheaper than what they think. It'd be good for all of us involved."

I push my sunglasses further up onto my head so I can see the iPad, inputting the data and uploading it to the cloud so Justin can see in real-time what's going on. Reed is always thinking of how he can benefit us and how we can benefit him. Cross promotion has been key to all of our businesses' growth, and he was the mastermind behind all that. "Sure."

"I want to thank you for what you did last night." He gives me a sweet smile as we walk along the grass line towards the front yard.

Dear Jesus, that smile. It breaks apart his tan face, and I know if he wasn't sporting a semi-beard I'd see a dimple in the right cheek. "It wasn't a big deal, Reed. I'll do whatever it takes to help out a friend. You know that, but I do have to warn you…I had a talk with Justin this morning, and he isn't happy with either of us." Little does he know that's putting it mildly.

He laughs, setting his hands on his hips, inadvertently show-casing how trim they are. I want to wrap my legs around them at some point. I almost guarantee they're strong enough to hold me up on their own. I scold myself to stop this line of thinking; it's going to get me nowhere.

"I know, I got a text from him. First thing he said was he reserves the right to kick my ass. Which is fine. Had I thought it through last night, I probably would have warned you this isn't worth it, but we've started now, and since Lacey knows, there's no reason for us to stop. He also advised me to be careful with you, because you worm your way into people's lives, and before you know it, they want you around all the time."

I fucking wish for that to happen more than I've ever wished anything in my life. "Either that, or I annoy the shit outta you." I flash him my own smile. I wonder for a minute if he's flirting, but no, Reed has never flirted with me, and if he's doing it now, it's so other people will see or hear it.

That's what I have to keep telling myself. Right now none of this is real, no matter how much I wish it was. Reality versus fiction is the name of this game, and I have to keep my heart locked tight. He could shatter it into a thousand tiny pieces.

Reed

AM I REALLY flirting with her? The honest answer to myself? Yes. Fuck yes. I haven't been able to take my eyes off her ass since she started squatting down to check her measurements. Then she went on her knees like she would straddle some lucky dude at his hips, and I just about combusted. I have to keep telling myself she's not really mine, but I'm a monogamous guy, and maybe this was a bad fucking idea. I've never been the kind of guy who can flit from woman to woman. Even when I was a kid, I needed that long-term relationship. I want to put my ring on a woman's finger. I want to give her my last name. It's ingrained in me.

We come around the house, and I tuck her into my side, putting my arm around her neck. The guys were already watching her, and I'll be damned, if it's fake or not, I'm staking a claim on her. I turn my face into the bend of her shoulder and place a kiss on her cheek.

"Reed." She giggles, but it's breathless, and I wonder if she feels what I do. When she stepped down from the truck and I saw her, my stomach flipped, my heart pounded. I haven't felt the reaction in a long time, and I'm trying to figure out why I do now. Why her, what's changed? It's never been like that with her before.

Is it me? Have I started to move on, in my own way? Lacey and I haven't been together for a year, and I've stopped looking for her in the house, I've stopped laying out enough dinner for two people, I've quit almost calling her when I'm going to be late at night. But Sass, I shake my head to myself. Where the fuck did she come from?

"What?" I ask, laughing softly with her.

"You don't have to do things you don't want to do in order to make people think we're together. We could call it a fling."

I know right now Sass will never be a fling kind of woman, and in our small town, there are rumors that go along with flings. She's about as into a fling as I am—there are warning signs here, but I'm choosing to ignore them. I won't acknowledge how long we've known each other, or how much she's grown up, or how she looks at me like I hang her whole world sometimes. "Would it be crazy if I said I wanna have fun with you? There's no expectation with you Sass. You know most of what I've done in my life. I don't have to worry about being somebody I'm not with you. Would it be so bad?"

She's breathing heavily, like she's run a marathon. "No." She shakes her head. "It wouldn't be bad. We're friends, right?"

And at this point, I'm thinking I might like to be more than that with her. "Yeah, we are."

"Then let's be friends," she grins, "and see where it goes."

It's been a long time since I let fate decide my path, but I think back. The last time I did it was when I took out a loan for my own construction company I knew I'd never be able to pay back, and I haven't looked back since. Maybe this isn't such a bad thing, and maybe I should stop overthinking everything in my life. It got me nowhere with Lacey.

"Alright," I agree, wondering if this is a good idea or not.

"Good." She smiles up at me. "Now help me finish these measurements so I can move on to the next jobsite. I think in celebration of us being friends, you should totally cook me dinner in your outdoor kitchen. With the heat the way it is, my apartment will melt."

"You're somethin' else." I shake my head. "But you're on. Be there at seven."

This was either the best decision of my life, or the worst mistake. Unfortunately, we never know until the situation we're in ends. Sooner or later, I'll find out.

CHAPTER FIVE

Reed

*T*HIS ISN'T A *date*, I keep telling myself. I don't have to try and impress Sass. We're friends, not lovers. But something pulls at the edges of my subconscious. It tells me I want to impress her; I want to be the person who shows her a good time. I don't know her past experiences—she's kept quiet from both me and Justin—probably because she knew we'd do nothing more than tease and make fun. That's what brothers and brothers' best friends do. Now, I find myself wanting to know. Who has she had? What has she done? Have they treated her well? Has she had someone like me? Has she ever been serious with anyone the way I was with Lacey?

Fuck, I even looked over my clothes, deciding on a blue T-shirt in the style of the white one I wore this afternoon. I'd have to be blind not to see the way she had been staring at me. She'd licked her lips every time my shirt had stuck to my abs. I'd be lying if I said that hadn't given me a little thrill. I'm not ashamed to say after Lacey cheated on me, I did have a few months where I wondered if I wasn't a good-looking guy, if I wasn't enough to keep a woman satisfied. I'm not entirely over that yet, so knowing she'd enjoyed the way I looked this afternoon meant a hell of a lot to me. It doesn't escape me that I'm dressed completely different than I used to dress when I'd go out on a date with Lacey. Even though I'm steaks and beer, Lacey never saw me that way. She always wanted me to look like the businessman I am.

"Oh for goodness sakes, Reed. Look like you own your own company when we go out." Lacey rolls her eyes as she gets a look at me.

It's been a long day. Nothing has gone right, and all I want to do is go out with my woman, our friends, and throw back a couple of longnecks. "What's wrong with this?" I look down at my University of Alabama T-shirt and jeans. Yeah, the jeans have a hole or two in them, but they're comfortable, and right now I'm all about comfort.

"Look at me, Reed. How do you think we'll look together?" She purses her lips at me. It's a look I've seen more than once and will probably see many more times. She wears my ring now, and next year she'll take my last name. I take a deep breath. Do I really want to argue about this tonight?

Doing as she asks, I take a good look at her. Her hair is perfectly curled, her makeup is caked on, and the sundress she wears shows off tan legs she's gotten by lounging around her parents' pool. She looks impeccable.

"I've had a long day, Lace, and to be honest I could give two flyin' fucks what anyone says about what I'm wearing. If it's that big a deal, they don't have to look at me."

Immediately I know I've said the wrong thing, but this is one time she's not going to make me go change. I've done it too many times in this relationship to make her happy. Tonight I'm going to be happy.

"Reed, really?"

"Yeah, really. I don't talk about the way you can't leave the house without makeup on. I'm gonna be comfortable tonight; you can suck it up, sweetheart, or stay here."

She mumbles as she pushes past me, opting to get into her car instead of my truck. It's a rebellious act and we both know it. She's been on me for months to stop working on my job sites and to get rid of my truck. It's an argument we've been having, but I refuse to give up everything that makes me, me.

The doorbell rings, breaking me from my memories. I grab my phone out of my pocket, checking the time. Just like Sass, right on the dot. I appreciate that about her. Lacey was usually at least ten minutes late—at the end of our relationship, I'd taken to giving her the wrong times. Otherwise, I'd be waiting, and if there's one thing I hate, it's to wait. I take the stairs two at a time, and within seconds, I'm at the front door. Opening it, my mouth falls open as I take in the woman standing in front of me.

There's a resistance from me, I have to explain about Sass. She's always been Justin's sister. Before the other day, I never saw her as anything more than that. Well, that's kind of a lie. There was the day I realized she wasn't a little kid anymore, but I took those thoughts and locked them in a vault. One that I never knew the code to unlock. I wouldn't allow myself, because I didn't want to mess up the friendships I have. "Off limits" is a good way to describe her, and I never went there with her, but *fuck me*, now I've kind of given myself permission to go there, I know one truth. I'm in deep shit. I'm not sure I can close the vault again or give back that code.

"You look…" I trail off, because there aren't enough words for me to describe how she looks. My high school education isn't helping me either, so I open the door further and let her in. Sass has always been a cute girl, good-looking chick, and now she's grown into a gorgeous woman. Not too tall, not too short, but legs that go on for miles—her head hits me at my collar bone. I like her that way. Her hair is bleached by the sun, making her blue eyes stand out in stark contrast. For the first time I notice how plump her lips are, looking like they've been stung by a bee all the time. I wonder why I've never noticed that before. But what she's wearing, God above.

A baby blue sundress shows off the tan she's gotten over the summer, making her skin glow. I've never seen her look this way before. When we go out to the bar, it's tank tops and ripped jeans, or a long sweater and leggings. Of course I've seen her in a swimsuit, but there's something about seeing her in this sundress, giving me little glimpses of skin as she moves. She's left her hair curly tonight, pulling it back at the nape of her neck.

That neck, holy shit. I never noticed how long and graceful it was before, and I'm totally a neck man. It's begging for my lips, and it takes everything I have not to forego this meal I'm cooking for us and make her my dessert. Flip flops cover her feet, and that is traditional Sass. If she's able to wear flip flops, that's what she's gonna wear.

"Thanks." She grins up at me. "You don't look so bad yourself. Too bad I didn't have a dark blue sundress, then we could have matched."

I don't miss the way her eyes roam my body. The same way they did earlier today. Score one for my self-esteem, as much as I pretend I don't need it. I do. Don't we all?

"Next time," I offer. "I need to check on the grill. I turned it on a few minutes ago. It should be warm enough by now."

I motion for her to walk in front of me; not because I'm being a gentleman, but because I want to watch her ass shake. I'm not disappointed in that either. Another difference between her and Lacey. Lacey didn't like showing herself off to me, and now I know why. She was showing herself off to other men. I know Sass, though, probably better than she knows herself. She shows only what she wants to, and to know she wants to show herself off to me, when no one else is around—means everything. It takes my breath, to be honest.

"What are you cooking?" she asks over her shoulder, grinning as she catches me watching her. Her eyes sparkle, and right now I'll do whatever it takes to put that sparkle in them whenever I can.

"Steak, baked potatoes, I might have a salad in here some-where if you require some leafy green vegetables."

She throws her head back, laughing. "It all depends on what kind of dressing you got, because if it's that honey mustard shit you like, I'll enjoy eatin' only meat and potatoes."

The words "eatin' meat" go straight to my groin, and I know that's not what she meant at all. "Have a seat."

She does, and I turn towards the grill, checking the heat, welcoming the break I have from the way her body looks and the way her eyes stare at me. They see absolutely everything, and it unnerves me in a way I can't explain. I'm being laid out bare, and this isn't what I'm used to, someone who pays attention to me like this.

Sass

REED IS KILLING me. It's like he knew exactly what I loved about what he was wearing today and decided to go in for the kill tonight. I cross my legs as I have a seat at the outdoor table, welcoming the way the ceiling fans move the air around me. It's feels almost as if it's caressing my skin, and I can't help but notice the tension between Reed and me. It's been there before, at least on my part, but I've never noticed it from him. Some-thing has changed with him, and I'm not sure what, but I like it. I have hope maybe in the end this won't be one-sided, but I try to tell myself not to ruin this before it starts. To take this as it comes and not force anything, but my heart is having a hard time telling my brain that. After all, my heart has been involved in this for at least ten years.

"You cook for women often?" I flirt, flashing him what I've been informed is my best smile.

When I was a waitress, this particular smile won me the best tips. Those tips put me through school and gave me spending money while I was in college. I was damn good at my job, and I can flirt with the best of them.

"Only for you, Sass." He turns around, winking at me, before turning back towards the grill. "How do you want your steak?"

Telling myself not to look too far into the comment about him only cooking for me, I do my best to answer in a voice that's normal and not the voice of a teenager at a One Direction concert.

"Dead," I quip. "Unlike you."

"Hey," he argues. "The taste when it's still pink in the center is mouthwatering."

"Pink? That thing is still like living on your plate when you eat it. I'm surprised it's not breathing."

He laughs, and it's a sound I haven't heard much of in the last few months. It makes my heart happy. I want to make him laugh more often; I want to make him enjoy himself. I want to make him enjoy me.

I decide in that moment I want to be the reason he smiles— and damn anyone who stands in my way. It doesn't matter how hard it is, it doesn't matter how much it might hurt me. I want to be his reason—fuck it—I *will* be his reason.

CHAPTER SIX

Sass

I'M LOOKING FOR a distraction, and this is the first time I've seen his outdoor kitchen. I've obviously heard him talk about it as he was building it, because he'd been so excited about it. His anxious rambling about it, though, was nothing compared to what it looks like in person. It's going to be perfect as we get deeper into the summer. This will be the perfect place for the group of us to have cookouts and hang out together. We haven't done that in a long time because Lacey didn't like us hanging around. That should have been his first clue she wasn't for him. The cool breeze off of his pool is being distributed by the overhead ceiling fans, and I lift my face up, welcoming the chill. I need something to cool me down before I disintegrate into a pile of mush right here.

No other man has ever cooked for me, and seeing him do it warms a spot in my heart. Would this be what our nights were like if we were together permanently? He'd come home from work, I'd come home from work, and we'd congregate out here. He'd cook dinner, I'd do the dishes, and then we could either end up in the pool or in the living room on the couch, Netflix and chilling? I feel goosebumps on my skin thinking about it. I wonder if I'm putting the cart before the horse, so to speak, but I can't help it. The thoughts wonder in, they grow root, and they take hold.

If I had cooked in my apartment, the paramedics would be there right now, treating me for a heat stroke, and I'm more than appreciative he took my suggestion to let me come over. He didn't realize it would give me more daydream material.

"This is really beautiful, Reed." I appreciate the hard work he's done. He takes pride in his work, and so many times no one tells him how it looks. They either give him a token "it looks great", or they pay him the money for the job. By all accounts that should be enough, but when you're a craftsman like Reed, I know he appreciates the words way more than the actions. Sometimes, I feel like he's the teenager I first knew, searching for approval he's never going to get. That's another thing too; I want to be his cheerleader, I want to be the person who tells him what an amazing job he's done. I don't ever want him to question whether he's good enough or not. Because he's one of the best.

"Thanks." He flashes me a pleased look, appreciation in his eyes that I've taken the time to do that. "I laid all the stonework myself too." He indicates the outdoor kitchen. From what I can see, it has a grill, a countertop stove, a fridge, a freezer, and a drink station.

"You're talented. Way more talented than any of us give you credit for." I praise him because he deserves it, and I'm not sure any of us have ever done that for him. Sure, we all know he works hard, but he's kind of an artist too, and I know that personally I never noticed it. I bet none of our other friends have either.

The only pieces of stainless steel equipment are the grill and a refrigerator. "Have you always wanted one of these?" I ask, because I know I've always wanted an outdoor kitchen. I hate cooking in the heat, but I've never had the space, money, or a guy who would help me build it. While I can do lots of things on my own, building a space like this isn't one of them.

He nods. "It gets so hot in houses, even with air conditioning down here in the summer. If you don't have a good air conditioner, it puts so much strain on it. This is a build I've wanted to do a long time. Plus," he adds, "I like grilled meat and vegetables. I have to make sure I'm in shape. My job is physically demanding, and if I'm not, I pay the price."

I take a look at his strong back through the thin shirt he's wearing and can tell he's a guy who spends time building up those muscles. They aren't huge, but they aren't small. They are well conditioned and very well proportioned to his body. He's not a muscle head, but he could carry me around if he needed to. Preferably to bed. I clear my throat.

"That's something I need to do." I stretch my legs out in front of me, putting my feet in the chair beside me. I make sure nothing is showing in the dress I'm wearing. "I was much more active as a waitress. Now I push a ton of paper and sit behind a desk. Things aren't as tight as they used to be." I smirk.

He turns around and runs his eyes over my bare legs. "You look mighty fine to me."

The deep timbre of his voice causes goosebumps to pop up on my body. It's a tone of voice he's never used with me before, and I can't help but want to put it in my pocket and hold it for later. It's the tone of voice I've heard him use when he's trying to seduce a woman. I haven't heard it in a long time, but I distinctly remember it from his and Justin's early years. My heart beats wildly in my chest. I've never in my life believed he would see me this way, but there's no mistaking the genuine interest in his gaze.

"Thanks." I give him a smile. "I need to start running again, but I haven't since high school. I've noticed my knees and legs snap, crackle, and pop when I do certain stuff on job sites. I need to take my conditioning more seriously."

"You were pretty kick-ass on that cross country team, though."

I can't believe he remembers; it's so long ago, and I never thought he paid attention.

"I was a cheerleader for my mama; I ran for myself. There's something about setting a pace and hearing your feet hit the pavement, or the dirt, or whatever. It's a control type thing. I control the pace, and I choose if I pick it up. It's almost therapeutic in a way."

I haven't paid attention to the fact he's done with the steaks, plating them both up with baked potatoes and it looks like grilled asparagus. "You wanna grab some beers?" he asks as he puts the plates on the table.

"Sure, they over here?" I indicate the outside fridge.

"Yeah, dessert's in there too, if you wanna take a look."

Now I'm curious. What kind of dessert could he have gotten? I have an extensive sweet tooth, so I'll be good with whatever, as long as pineapple isn't in it. Opening the door, I grab out the first two beers in the front, and then my eye catches it. It's a strawberry pie from the diner in town, and I want to marry this man right here, right now. "You got one?" I ask, my eyes wide.

Those pies are such a hot commodity you have to be there at opening, and it's a rare day I can get up, at 'em, and be somewhere at five in the morning.

"Yeah." He grins. "Nell," he mentions the name of the well-beloved cook, "kind of owed me a favor. I did some work on her house for free last year. Anytime I call and ask for a special order, she gets it to me."

"Well I'm excited." I grin as I sit down at the table and grab the Heinz 57 he's placed in front of me. I'm amazed at all the little nuances of mine he's noticed, and I try not to let my pulse skip when he refers to "something special" being the pie I know is just for me.

"I am too," he answers, and I can't help but believe he means it.

"It's been a long time since somebody cooked for me, so I'm gonna enjoy this."

My steak is sufficiently burnt, but it's still able to be chewed, and I'm pretty sure this man is the most perfect man in the world for me. I'm going to have to hang on to the heart that's currently trying to beat itself out of my chest. I'm going to have to be strong and realize this isn't for real.

Then he smiles at me from across the table before he takes a drink of his beer.

And I know it.

I'm dead.

He's got me.

I've got control of nothing.

CHAPTER SEVEN

Reed

TODAY HAS BEEN a shit day; nothing has gone according to plan. I haven't talked to Sass in the three days since she had dinner at the house, and it's put me in a foul mood. I don't even want to examine why it does, but I'm ready to bite someone's head off, chew it up, and spit it out. We've both been incredibly busy. I've been in meetings with a new developer who wants my company to oversee the builds of ten houses in a new planned community subdivision that's going to require me to hire ten more workers. It's stressful, and I'm hoping like hell I can afford it and it doesn't put me out of business. But I know I have to take a chance in order to make my business grow.

It's hard to know what's good business and a great opportunity compared to what will be the decision that leads us to ruin. That's a lot of pressure. I have a crew of guys who depend on me for their livelihood. They need me to put their kids through school, make their mortgage payment, or take family vacation. Sometimes that pressure is too much to bear. It weighs on me, and when I can feel the tension in my shoulders and back, I know I need a release. Right now that fucking tension is creeping up my shoulders. It's got to give, or it's going to break me.

Straight Edge is elbows deep, literally, in finishing up the landscaping on a new community center opening for the county. The ribbon cutting is today, and Sass sent me a picture of her planting flowers yesterday. They've even pulled in their mom to help.

My mood is fucking foul. It's been a hot one, I worked my ass off, and I seriously want to be at home, in my pool, swimming away this frustration. Instead, my truck is almost out of gas, and I'm sitting in a line three deep at the local convenience store, waiting to fill up. I'm beyond irritated when I finally pull up to the pump and get out so I can get this chore over with and go home.

"Hey, hot stuff."

I grin, because Sass' voice is on the other side of the pump.

Putting the nozzle into my truck and turning the pump on, I fix it so that it automatically runs and then step over the concrete curb, positioning myself to see the person speaking to me. "Hey, yourself." I get a good look at her.

Her hair is falling down from a ponytail, her shirt and cut-off shorts have obviously seen better days. They are covered in dirt, her legs have traces of dirt on them, and there's even a smudge on her face. "Rough day?" I ask. I get the feeling maybe she's had one like mine.

"The worst." She puts her aviator sunglasses on the top of her head, and I can see her eyes are red-rimmed; she's obviously been crying.

This is where I should act the part of a concerned boyfriend, but there is no acting. Something is wrong with her, and it scares the fuck outta me. "Whose ass do I have to kick?" It strikes me hard in the chest that I mean it. Nobody is going to make her upset on my watch.

She laughs, rolling her eyes, but it brings about a fresh wave of wetness, because tears escape the corners and roll down her cheeks. Sass bites her lip and then lifts the side of her mouth up, flashing her white teeth. "It's stupid."

The tears are in her voice, and this is so foreign to me. Sass is the strongest woman I've ever met. My pump cuts off, and I look behind me, seeing the cars are still three deep, but fuck that. I step closer to her and grab her up into a hug. She digs her fingers into my arms as she holds tightly. I tighten mine around her, lifting her slightly off the ground with the force of the hug. Wetness comes through my shirt, and suddenly a car horn honks, breaking the moment we have. My rage wants to kill the fucker, but my concern for her trumps my rage.

"Nothing that's got you this upset is stupid. I don't know about you, but I was thinking a swim in my pool would cure all the aches and pains of the day. Both physical and emotional." I cup her cheeks and use my thumbs to brush some of the wetness off her face. 1 can't help it, seeing her bare like this is killing me. "Come over."

"I don't know." She grabs her hair from behind her back and starts braiding it.

It's a nervous gesture she's had since she was a kid. It breaks my heart as much as the tears do. I don't want her to be nervous around me; I don't want her to feel like she has to hold her emotions in. Maybe this was a way I could have been there for Lacey more, and I don't want to fuck this up with Sass. It doesn't escape me I'm thinking long-term. I'm thinking about how to improve on the mistakes I made in my last relationship. I can't stop to examine that right now. She needs me, and I want to be there for her in a way I haven't been there for other women.

Maybe that's what makes her different. She's my friend, and she's been my friend for so long I immediately care about her feelings. I shake my head, because I don't know when I turned into my own shrink.

"Go home, grab some clothes and a swimsuit, take a shower, and come over." My voice is more forceful than I've ever used with her.

She sticks her hands into the pockets of her cut-offs and rocks back onto her heels. "I don't want to ruin your evening."

"Fuck that noise." I shake my head. "You'll make it better."

The car horn honks again, and I raise my hand to flip them off, not turning to look at them. Not caring what they want. Nothing is more important than what I'm doing right here, right now, and I want her to believe that. They can move to another fucking pump if they're in that damn big of a hurry. This is way more important to me. "Go ahead and say yes so we can let this douchebag have this gas pump. I'm not leaving until you give me the answer I want to hear."

Our eyes meet and she giggles. "Okay," she relents. "Do you want me to bring dinner?"

My stomach growls, and for the first time I realize how fucking hungry I am. "I'll pick up Chinese, is that good?"

"Yeah." She nods. "You know what I like."

We break apart, and she finishes her gas purchase, grabbing her receipt. Leaning up on her tiptoes, she brushes a kiss so soft I barely feel it against my lips. "Thanks for knowing what I need, Reed," she whispers before getting into her car.

She drives off, her taillights bright in the early evening light, and the asshole who's been honking at us pulls in and gets out. I level him with the stare I use when people are jerking me around with prices on materials, and he backs off. Stepping back over the concrete curb, I grab my own receipt and hop into my truck. After everything shitty that's gone on today, my night is definitely looking up.

CHAPTER EIGHT

Reed

S ITTING ACROSS FROM Sass, I give her a thorough once-over, making sure she's okay. Since she was a kid, I haven't been able to stand the tears. That was the main reason I stayed with her on the night of her dad's death, to make sure she was fine. I've never been completely fond of heights, but knowing that Justin had to take care of their mom, I knew someone had to take care of Sass, and I had known exactly where she would be. There've never been many people in my life for whom I would set aside my fear of heights, but Sass is one of them. Those are feelings I'm not sure I can examine right now, or that I even want to. Just thinking of them leaves me feeling open and exposed in a way I never have been before.

We sit outside, at the table in the outdoor kitchen. I can breathe easier here. I don't feel so cooped up, and the scenery calms me. The quiet gives me a peace I don't have anywhere else, and I realize sitting here enjoying it all with Sass makes me happier than I've been in a long time.

Looking at her, I can still see the faded tracks of her tears, even though she's showered. I think she may have cried more on her way over, and probably in the shower too. She's always been a shower crier—hoping no one can hear her as she lets the water cleanse her soul. I remember hearing her for months after her dad died when I would stick around the house to help Justin. It broke my heart then, and it breaks my heart now.

I wish she would let me in and let me help soothe her on days like today. There's no reason she should be upset about anything.

"How's your bourbon chicken?" I ask as she grabs a piece before putting some sticky rice in her mouth.

"It's good." She gives me a fake smile, it breaks my heart.

"Don't bullshit me, Sass. How are you really doing?"

She stabs her chopsticks into the rice. "I'm fine. Right now, I don't want to talk about myself. Why don't we talk about you?"

This is a diversionary tactic and I know it. Obviously she's not ready to discuss completely what went down, and I respect that. I have too. "What do you want to talk about?"

"What had you so wound up earlier?"

I grab a piece of my sweet and sour chicken with my own chopsticks and shove it into my mouth to give myself time to formulate the answer to her question. There are many times when I'm not free to speak about what's going on in my business life, and there were many times with Lacey where she didn't want to hear about it.

"Why are you being such an ass tonight, Reed?"

I don't mean to be an ass, but I'm worried about the job I'm working on right now. In order to come in under budget, we're going to have to cut some corners, and it's times like these I hate that the market dictates so much of my job.

"Babe, I don't mean to be an ass." I pull Lacey into my arms. She sighs and snuggles closer to me. "The price on marble and granite are going up—up by more than they were when I first put in my bid on this job. I'm worried we won't make the profit we need to. If we don't make the profit we need to, then payroll might not be met, and I'll have to dip into some of the liquid assets for the business," I explain.

She's quiet for a few minutes. "This is why I like working for myself and by myself. Does this mean we won't be able to go to Gulf Shores in a few weeks?"

Seriously? I've just explained to her I might need to dip into savings to pay my guys, and she's worried about if we're going on vacation. When she does this type of shit, it kills me because I know she's more than this. "Don't worry, Lace, you'll get your fucking vacation."

"Don't talk to me like that." She pulls back. "We've been working our asses off for the past year. We deserve this."

It strikes me that the Lacey of a few years ago would have never said she deserved anything. As my business has gotten more popular and hers has gotten more solvent and able to sustain a certain amount of income, her tastes have gotten more extravagant. I'm not saying mine haven't—but fuck I still keep Ramen in the truck on the off-chance I need to eat it.

"And I'm not saying we haven't been, Lace, but what if this continues and I have to lay off workers to remain solvent? It's a fear I have every job." But she doesn't want to hear that, because she's stuck in her own little world she's made for herself.

"That's your problem, Reed, not mine."

"You okay?" Sass asks, interrupting my thoughts. Not everything with Lacey was bad, obviously not if I was going to marry her, but the fact I'm being made to face some hard truths reminds me that not everything was good either. I'm no longer looking at my situation with rose-colored glasses. It's the biggest wake-up call I've ever had. The woman I was spending all my time missing was also a person who drove me nuts on a semi-regular basis.

"Yeah." I clear my throat, wondering how much I want to share with Sass. I get the distinct feeling Sass would understand. She would sympathize with where I'm coming from, and the two of us would be a unit. "I met with a developer today, and he wants me to oversee a new subdivision over on Hidden Creek. It will start with ten houses that will eventually be part of a pre-planned community. In order for me to meet his deadline, I'm going to have to take on ten workers. While I know it's for the better of the company, and right now Spartan County is seeing the kind of growth we haven't seen in decades, I'm worried the strain on the company will be too much."

"Like you won't pull the profit margin?" she asks as she takes a drink of her Corona.

She fucking gets it already. "Exactly. While RS Construction is doing well, we still have a small margin with which to play with. Materials, delivery charges, or gas goes up too much too quickly, there's not a snowball's chance in hell I can stop the bleeding quick enough to keep on all the employees I have plus the new ones I'm gonna have to hire. That shit keeps me up at night."

"Justin and I talk about that a lot. It's a delicate balance not many people understand. You hold people's lives and livelihood in your hands."

I nod as I take a drink of my own Corona. "I feel that responsibility too. Lacey always said I took it more seriously than I should."

Sass rolls her eyes. "The only thing she felt was her nail when it broke. You're a good businessman, Reed; that's why you worry about it. You're excellent at what you do, and I know you'll work this out, however it needs to be worked out. You know Justin and I have your back and will help you with whatever you need."

That was the amazing thing about my friends, they would. They'd even help me hang drywall if I needed it. "I know." I roll my shoulders to release some of the tension that's seeped in while we've been talking. "Right now, we need to have a swim, wash all this tension and doubt away."

I get up from the table and hold my hand out to her. "What do you say, Sass?"

There is no hesitation. She puts her hand in mine, and I know it's that blind trust that's going to be my undoing.

CHAPTER NINE

Sass

REED HAD THE right idea when he suggested I use his pool. The water washing over my body is taking away all the stress of the day and leaving me with a much calmer feeling. Even the upset part of me is feeling better, and life doesn't look so glum now. I hate when Justin and I fight. It's even more unusual the older we get, and this time was a real doozy. I try to push those thoughts out of my head—this is supposed to be relaxing me. As I lean to the left, I suck in a breath of air and stroke further down the pool. Having swam out most of my aggression and frustration, I stop and lean against the side of the pool, trying to catch my breath. Swimming is a good workout, and I should probably do it more often.

Reed is watching me; I can feel it deep down in my bones. His eyes have followed me the entire time I've been in the water. It's unnerving, but at the same time, I welcome his eyes on me. There's a part of me that wishes I knew what he sees when he looks at me like this. His eyes are soft, like he can see right through me, like he knows more than I want him to. It's not like I'm a closed off book, but I don't let many people get too close. Justin, Morgan, and that's about it besides my mom and Reed. It's a leftover feeling from when my dad died. If people aren't close, it can't hurt when they leave.

"Good idea?" he asks, pushing off his wall and treading towards me. The pool isn't huge, and it doesn't take him long to get over to me. I dip my head in the water to push my hair back from my face. It surprises the hell out of me when he puts his arms around my waist and supports my back, bringing me up so I'm face to face with him.

"What made you cry earlier?" he asks out of the blue. I figured he wouldn't press; he knows I'm the type of person to keep things in, but here he is asking me, not letting me get too deep inside my own head.

There's a part of me that doesn't want to tell him. This is family business, but Reed is nothing if not family, and I'm comfortable with him. I also know he doesn't blindly take my brother's side in everything. He's fair and listens. "It was Justin," I admit, thinking back to the argument the two of us had.

"The fucking account is overdrawn now, Cassandra. These are things we can't let happen. Fuck, this has never happened in the years I've owned this business. You should have been paying more attention." He slams the piece of paper from the bank down on the desk.

I'm in shock, because I didn't even know this bill was coming out of the account, and I'm frantically trying to find the invoice. "I don't know what happened." My voice is small and I hate it, but I also hate to disappoint my brother. The three guys who walked in with him are trying hard not to look at me; they're trying to make their way out of the office when they realize how personal this is. I'm trying hard not to let my anger come through as I realize he's going at me in front of our employees.

"You better figure it out. I'm on my way now to move money. Thank God Morgan works there and she called me. I got her call before I got the letter." He slams his hat back on his head. "You can't make mistakes like this and still pay our employees. Figure it the fuck out."

I jump as he slams the office door, still trying to figure out where the invoice even came from. I hate when he yells at me, it's like my dad yelling at me. Disappointing him kills me, and I take a deep breath, willing my fingers to stop shaking. I'm going to find the invoice that caused the overdraft, even if it kills me. When his truck starts up, I let the tears fall. I won't let him see me cry, but I know they have to escape, I know I have to let the emotion out. I allow myself five minutes, and then I square my shoulders, resolving to fix this.

Reed nods after I recount the details to him. "Somehow that doesn't surprise me."

"Normally we can work together just fine. I mean we've been brother and sister for twenty-four years." I give him a cheeky grin. "But sometimes he can get to me, and he's not always nice when he does."

He pushes us towards the wall until my back hits it and he's crowding me. I'm enveloped by his heat, surprised by my reaction towards him. I want to curl up in a ball and ask him to hold me until this is all better. His voice is soft but firm when he makes his request. "Wanna tell me what happened?"

He's not going to let this go. In his eyes I see he truly wants to know, but this feels too intimate. It feels like a real relationship. I have to remind myself it isn't what it seems. I have to warn my stupid heart that he's being a friend, and that's all. He cares because he's known me most of my life, and if anyone understands what a dick Justin can be, it's Reed. Still, I open my mouth and the words rush out.

"I made a mistake," I admit, my voice small. "To be fair though, it was because of him and his fucked up filing system."

He brushes my hair back from my face so he can look at me. His eyes are dark with an understanding I haven't received all day, and it almost makes me want to cry again. "Everybody makes mistakes, especially when you first start working for a family business. There are things you have to learn, just like you'd have to learn anywhere else. The bad part is everyone expects you to be perfect from the get-go, and that's not feasible in some instances."

"Right?" I sigh. "A bill was due, and I didn't enter it because it wasn't in my invoices. I didn't know Justin gets this one emailed to the company email address. I didn't know to look for it," I defend myself. "I saw it, but I didn't realize what it was. Maybe I should have asked." My voice trails off.

I lean into him when his arms tighten around my waist, his big hands trailing up and down my back in a comforting rhythm. His voice is soft when he asks the question I've been waiting on. "Was it ugly? I know how he can be."

I let out a laugh, because with Reed I can be myself. I don't have to be the tough girl. He sees me as a woman, not as a sister who shouldn't disturb anything and who should know all of the ins and outs without having truly been explained them. "Ugly doesn't even begin to describe it. He berated me in front of a crew because he'd assumed the bill was paid and used the money on something else. Now there's an overdraft on the account, so he had to go to the bank and take out savings to cover it. I had Morgan move what he took out of the company savings back from my own savings account, so there's not a shortage. It was the most embarrassing thing I've ever had to go in there and do. That's why I was crying when you saw me. All the other customers were looking at me, like they knew what kind of mistake I made. Morgan even looked at me as if I were a pitiful little kid. I can do this," I continue. I want him to see I'm an adult; I don't want to feel this small and stupid around him. "I can make sure the business runs smoothly, but I also have to be informed of all the bills," I defend myself.

His warm hands tighten around me, the tips grazing the waistband of my bikini bottoms. There's pity in his gaze, and I hate it. I hate that he's looking at me like I'm having a nervous breakdown. When in reality I'm upset and disappointed. "Sass, you shouldn't have done that. You shouldn't have moved your personal money unless it was absolutely the only way to keep you solvent. And it wasn't. When you make a mistake, you can't bail the business out, because there's usually an account just for those instances. If we moved money every time our businesses had a shortage, we'd all be broke. It comes out in the wash."

It's hard to explain, even to this man who's seen our family at its worst and its best. "I did. Justin helped put me through school; he made sure I did what I wanted to do, and I never had to want for anything growing up. After dad died, he sacrificed everything. The least I could do was take care of a mistake I made, but the way he handled it hurt, and it was embarrassing. How do I face those guys again?"

"He did all of those things for you because he wanted to," he argues, shaking his head at me. "Justin might want you to look at him like he's a martyr, but he took the responsibility on himself. No one ever asked him to." He boxes me in by moving his hands up to the concrete edge of the pool deck. Leaning in, he nuzzles my neck with his nose and mouth. Moving up towards my ear, his voice is soft. "Now, taking it out in front of a crew, that was wrong, he should have kept the argument between the two of you."

My stomach flutters as he breathes hot against my skin. We've never been this close physically before, and it's doing things to me. My nipples tighten against the top of my swimsuit, and since this is a serious conversation we're having, I hope he can't see it. My body has wanted this for a long time, and the touches he's freely giving me are driving me nuts.

"It doesn't make me feel any better." Because the fact of the matter is I was spoiled as a kid by my brother, and as an adult, I still am. To know I put him in financial difficulty makes me sad, like I'm even more of a burden.

"Don't take that on yourself, please don't," Reed continues. "Justin can be a mean son of a bitch when he wants to be. To get in your face in front of a crew pisses me off. There is going to be a time when he's gonna need your help, and you're gonna need to lead that crew. Him yelling at you in front of them gives them the right to talk to you in the same way. He fuckin' knows better than that."

I can see how this is going go. Reed's gonna run his mouth to Justin, and then Justin will assume I've run to his best friend and talked shit about him. That's not what I wanted at all; I wanted to say my piece and be done with it. "Please don't run to Justin and start shit. It's not at all what I wanted. I just wanted you to listen and see my side of things. I don't want you and Justin to get into an argument over me." I put my hand in his, twining our fingers together, hoping the touch centers and grounds us both.

He looks at me, his eyes growing darker. I've never seen him look at me this way, and I'm not sure how to respond to it, I don't know what it means.

His voice is low. "What exactly do you want, Sass?"

A part of me knows what he's asking; the other part of me isn't sure. Deciding to throw caution, I cup my hands around his cheeks and pull his chin down so we're almost to eye level. "What I want is to forget this shit day I've had. Can you help me with that?"

I can see him fighting what I'm asking. He's going over it in his mind, back and forth. I don't want him to do that. There's been an undercurrent of something between us, and I want to know what it is. Unconsciously, I lick my lips. His eyes lock on my tongue as he mumbles *son of a bitch* under his breath, and before my question is answered, his lips capture mine. It's the hottest kiss I've ever experienced in my life. It starts off slow, with no tongue, and that in itself is erotic, because I want it so much. Then with the barest of touches, he starts to inch his way in, testing the waters to see if I'm going to relax and let it go. Relaxing is the furthest thing from my mind, but I force my body to live in the moment. My legs hook tighter around his waist, digging my heels into his ass and pushing his cock harder against the bottoms I'm wearing. I want more, and I want him to claim me, imprint me, make sure anyone else who looks knows I'm his. Finally, when he takes full possession, I'm gripping his hair between my fingers and kissing him back with all the passion he's giving me.

CHAPTER TEN

Reed

NEVER IN MY life have I heated up as quickly as I do when Sass opens her mouth and lets me explore. Her fingers grip my cheeks, bringing my lips closer to hers, pressing them tightly together before abandoning my skin and delving deep into my hair. Her fingertips grip tightly at the ends of my hair as she presses herself roughly against my body; the tiny points her nipples make under her bikini top rub against my chest.

"You want this?" I ask her, needing to hear it from her, needing to make sure I'm not forcing her into something. It's been a while for me, and I'm more eager than I normally would be, but I have to remind myself who this is. I try not to let myself think about how this is going to affect our friendship. I'm only thinking about how good this is going to feel for both of us. Noticing her as I have for the past few days has been hell on my libido, and I want her more than I've even admitted to myself.

In a move I never would have anticipated from her, she runs her lips along my jawline and nips my earlobe with her teeth. My dick jumps at the sensation. "I've always wanted this." Her voice is as husky as I've ever heard it.

I halfway know what she means, and it causes my stomach to tighten at the implication, but I brush it aside, telling myself it doesn't matter. Fuck it, I know exactly what she means. She's wanted me since she was a fourteen-year-old kid. For ten years she's looked at me as if I've hung the moon and the stars. Today, tonight, I'm playing catch-up. There's a desire in her eyes I've never seen; or maybe I haven't wanted to see it, because I knew if I let myself acknowledge it, I'd have to admit that Sass wasn't a little girl anymore. There is absolutely no doubt in my mind as she presses against me; she's all woman now.

Grasping her roughly by the neck, I pull her lips back to mine as her legs encircle my waist.

Kissing someone has never been this all-consuming before. The two of us could explode at any minute with the sparks going between us. It's electricity without the static, the fire without the bomb. It's hot and passionate. Scary and volatile, like we can light up the midnight sky. I can't tell if it's the fact that maybe something has been brewing between the two of us since we started this charade or if it's the fact we've both had bad days. Part of me doesn't want to think about it and what it may mean for my friendship not only with her but with Justin as well.

She pulls her lips from mine, and we both breathe heavily, sharing the space in between our lips. "Do something to me," she begs, arching her body towards mine.

It's as if I've been in a slumber and those words awaken me. She's offering herself up on a platter, and I'd be a dumbass not to act. I push my hands down her back to where the bikini top is tied at the middle. I've never been this nervous when it comes to this part of a physical relationship, but I notice my hands are shaking, my fingers are clumsy. It's almost embarrassing how much I want her right now. It's a foreign feeling to me, because I have never had this mad dash, this all-consuming feeling before.

"I'm normally much smoother than this," I whisper against her lips, apologizing for my less than stellar performance on getting this top untied.

She throws her head back and laughs. It hits me right in the gut again—this is why I'm so enthralled by this woman. She lives life at a hundred miles an hour and appreciates everything it brings her. She loves the funny, appreciates the smart-ass, and lives for the sassy. There's nothing this woman takes for granted—she loves it *all*.

She reaches in, grabbing my lips with hers in a short kiss. "It's okay, I'm kind of nervous too."

Hearing the admission makes me want to make this the best experience she's ever had. I finally untangle the bikini strap and pull it down, exposing her chest to my eyes for the first time. Her tits are more than a handful and lie almost against her chest. She's blessed. Her nipples are tight against the coolness of the pool and the breeze of the night.

I harden, even in the cold water. Of its own mind, my mouth leans down and captures one of those taut nipples in my mouth, worrying the nub between my teeth. Her feet and fingers dig roughly into my body. Her fingers into my shoulders, her feet into my ass, shoving my erection against the cradle she's made of her pussy. Those fingers walk up the tendons of my neck and tangle in the strands of my hair. She shoves herself further into my mouth by arching her back and offering herself to me. It's the hottest thing she's ever done. I've never seen Sass like this before; I've always tried to keep her and thoughts of sex separate. This is more than I can handle.

Trailing my hands down her body, I grip the sides of her bottoms, untying them. "Push my swim trunks down and take my cock out." The words are a command I won't take back. Regardless of the fact I'm worried about what this means when I'm in her hand. I'm already hanging on by a thread, but I have to feel *her*.

She exhales sharply before reaching down, her small hand snaking into the waistband of my trunks and pushing them below my balls, taking my cock into her palm. I breathe deeply and throw my head back as she wraps her hands around me tightly, jacking it up and down without me even having to ask her.

"Reed." She sighs, resting her forehead in the curve of my shoulder.

"I know." The emotion clogs my throat and makes it hard to speak; it's never meant this much, it's a scary thought. Moving her thighs wider apart, I let her hand continue stroking me for a few minutes. "Put me inside you," I grind out, my lips tight against my teeth.

"I'm on birth control." She breathes out as she envelopes my length, moaning when I push myself home.

Fuck, I hadn't even asked, didn't even care, but now I want to know why. Has she had a lot of men? Female issues? All of a sudden, it's important to me. Am I up against an extensive list? "Because you're very active?"

"What?" She pulls back slightly. "No, because it keeps me regular." She laughs. "Trust me, I haven't been with a lot of men, but I'm hoping to be a lot more active with you."

I'm gone as her tight heat grips my length. It's a superhuman effort for me to withdraw and then push back in.

"Ah," she whines, grinding herself back against me.

This is everything I hoped it would be but never thought I'd find. Gripping her ass in my fingers, I push her harshly back towards me, sliding inside again.

We move in an unyielding rhythm. The only sound is our breath gusting out at one another and the lapping of the water from the pool. My abdomen tightens, and I know this isn't going to last much longer, I know I'm almost done for, and I want her to come with me.

Taking one of my hands, I move it down to the middle of her body and use my thumb to work her clit roughly. "What will get you there?" I ask, because I don't know all the nuances of her body yet. This is our first time, and I'm going to love learning. I'll dedicate my life to fucking learning.

"Your mouth, on my nipples, and don't go easy either." She pushes me towards them.

With pleasure. She likes it a little rough? I can give it to her a little rough. Using my tongue and my teeth, I do just that, pressing my cock deeply into her, crowding her against the side of the pool, thrusting into her deeply as I spread her legs even further with my body. She grinds against me, and it's like we have this symphony going with no music playing. I thrust, she grinds, I press against her clit, she nips my shoulder, I bite her nipple, and she sighs. It's everything I've never had before, a wild rush to a finish line I wasn't even sure we were racing towards. Then it hits me out of nowhere. An orgasm that has me groaning and gritting my teeth, hoping like hell I don't pass out from the pleasure.

"Fuck, Cassandra," I call her by her given name for the first time in years. In this emotionally charged moment she deserves it.

"I know." Her body detonates too.

I hold her tightly so she doesn't accidentally drown as she flails, riding out the waves of pleasure, when suddenly she slows and offers me a lazy smile. It hits me square in the chest, and I struggle to swallow against the feeling it gives me.

Who fucking knew the two of us would be like this together? I sure didn't, and it scares the absolute fuck outta me.

CHAPTER ELEVEN

Sass

M Y FACE FLAMES as I sit on the edge of Reed's bed, towel-drying my hair. After the pool, he suggested we move ourselves to the house and wash off the chlorine. At first I hadn't wanted to because it felt too much like he was inviting me to spend the night, and when he confirmed he was, I almost panicked. Then, I realized I better grab hold of this opportunity and take it—who knows how many more I'll have?

"Why are you blushing?" Reed chuckles at my embarrassment as he walks from the bathroom into the bedroom.

I wrinkle my nose up and offer him an indulgent smile of my own. "Because you're so damn hot. Like, can you bounce a quarter off those abs? It's nice." I giggle, and I can't believe I fucking giggled.

Now he's blushing, and I can't help but enjoy the smile on his face. It reminds me of when he was younger and didn't have the weight of the world on his shoulders. He looks carefree, and right now, we both kind of are. It's different between us than I assumed it would be.

Reaching forward, I grab his towel and pull him closer to my body bringing his crotch eye-level with me. Using my fingers, I move the towel down so his cock can escape. Taking it into my hand, I slide my palm up and down, against the softness of the skin. I shiver as he takes my towel off too, exposing my bare skin to the cool air.

"Fuck, Sass." He groans as he buries his fingers in my hair.

I lean forward, attempting to take his length in my mouth, but he yanks up firmly on my hair, forcing my eyes to meet his. There's something there I'm not sure about; it's dark, and it's almost as if he's fighting against memories.

"Don't." He shakes his head. "That's how I found her."

And suddenly I understand. This has everything to do with Lacey and nothing to do with me. That's fine, I'll let him run the show this time, but I want him inside my mouth, and I'll help him get over this phobia he appears to have. I won't force it, but I *will* make sure he knows this is what I want later.

He tilts my chin up with his hand and leans down, capturing my lips with his. If there's one thing Reed is good at, it's kissing. This one starts out lazy and slow, his tongue coaxing my mouth open as he slowly explores everything that is me. I wrap my arms around his waist, lightly scoring the tattoo he has on his ribcage with my fingers. The coolness of the necklace he wears—the St. Christopher medal—and he's had since I've known him trails against my chest. I know he's not devout, but I've never seen him take it off. For some reason, I feel as if it protects me too.

Pushing me back against the bed, he climbs over top of me, using his knees for leverage as he spreads my legs and lowers himself between them. He's hard at my center, pressing against me, but I don't want this to happen the same way it happened in the pool. Instead, I hook my foot around his leg and use my muscles to try to flip him over. We laugh as it halfway works.

"You want me on my back, sweetheart?" he asks, the endearment going straight to my chest.

I nod my head yes, because somewhere I've lost the ability to speak. I think it was the endearment. He chuckles as he moves himself up the bed and situates his back against the pillows. Laying his hands out to the side, he spreads his legs and shoots me a wink. "Come and get me."

In seconds, I'm on my knees, crawling up his body. I realize he doesn't want my mouth anywhere near his crotch, but I make a show of running my tongue up his abdomen, straight to his nipple, taking the taut flesh into my mouth and circling my tongue around it the same way he did with me earlier. His fingers hook around my ass, pulling me up so I sit against his length.

"What do you want, Reed?" I ask, because I want to know, I *need* to know. Does he see this as sex, or does he see it as me giving it to him? I'm all ears, and what's sad is I know the answer won't change anything about how I feel. No matter what he wants or how he feels, I know exactly how I do, and right now, this is what I want.

"You, Sass." He runs his hands up my stomach, using his thumbs to tease my nipples. "You," he breathes out. "I didn't know it, and I didn't realize how much I would want you, but I do."

I can tell by the way he's letting the words free of his throat he hadn't counted on this. He never meant to make our relationship physical, and right now I don't care. I wonder if tomorrow I'll wake up freaking out, but as he lifts me against his cock, I press down onto him, moaning. Whatever feelings I have in the morning I'll deal with. Living in the here and now is all I want; taking these chances and opportunities being presented to me is all I can wrap my head around.

Balancing on my knees, I lift up and back down; setting a rhythm between us that is slow but fast at the same time. I put my hands on his chest and use it to help my leverage. I'm moving back and forth against him, making sure my clit gets hit, because if there's something I've learned in the few sexual experiences I've had, it's that I want to take my own pleasure. I've never been able to hand it over to a man and hope to get mine. I think Reed, though, he would make sure I was taken care of, but right now—I want to take care of him.

His hands grip my ass and shove me down hard on top of him, so hard that I have to hook an arm up around his broad shoulders. Taking the upper hand, he flips me over so that I'm on my back.

"I let you play, baby, but now it's my turn."

My legs anchor around his waist, and I reach up, wrapping my hand around the wood of the headboard, using it to anchor my body as he pounds into me. Reed is stronger than I've given him credit for. There's sweat dripping off his face, but he's in a full pushup position over me, and he's swinging his hips wildly into me. His hands fist the sheets, and I wonder how long he can hold on. I wonder how long I can hold on as he moves one hand under my ass so he can push me closer to his body. I'm feeling every ridge of his muscles as I thrust up into him. The friction is there as I add a little grind to my thrust. Using the headboard, I arch my back and tilt my head, giving over every piece of myself to him. I'm wound tight as I seek my release, as I hold my breath and hope it comes sooner rather than later. His mouth latches onto my neck, and it's then I start to tighten and he does too.

"C'mon, Sass," he encourages me.

Letting go of the headboard with one hand, I move it down to where our bodies are joined and take my own pleasure, Reed following.

As we lay there, both catching our breaths, I wonder how in the world this is going to change our situation. It's the last thing on my mind as exhaustion pulls me under.

CHAPTER TWELVE

Sass

S OMETHING IS OFF as I awake from the best sleep I've had in what feels like years. I'm pressed up against a warmth that isn't the same as my mattress. The sounds are different too, they aren't the sounds of my apartment. I don't hear the window air unit or the loud-ass noise my fridge makes. Instead it's peaceful, except for the low hum of someone snoring almost in my ear.

Then it hits me. I'm not at home. I push my eyelids open, and sure enough, Reed is lying next to me. His arm is wrapped around my waist, his face buried in my hair. I turn over slowly, trying not to dislodge him so I can look at him. In sleep his face is much more relaxed than it is in everyday living. I can't get over the difference in the harsh lines that usually rest there. It amazes me how much those lines age him, but in sleep, he looks almost like a teenager.

Immediately I'm in a panic, because I remember what we did last night. Once in the pool, and then once we got back here to his bedroom. We laughed and we moaned, and it was the best experience I've ever had in my life. I remember what it meant to me, and I have a sneaking suspicion it meant nothing like that to him. The thought is enough to kill me, and my imagination is already running wild; it's making up scenarios in my head and freaking me the fuck out. My heart pounds as I realize what we've done, and I want to smack myself upside the head for letting my body rule instead of my head.

I have to get out of here. I can't let him wake up and see me here. He'll be able to look at my face and realize exactly what my feelings are, and I'm not sure if I'm ready for honesty like that yet. Scratch that, I know I'm not ready for it.

Quietly, I slip out of the bed, hoping I don't wake him up, and go around the room gathering up my clothing and putting on something appropriate for me to drive home in.

Ignoring the ache between my legs is difficult because it feels so delicious. I haven't been with many men, and none of them have consumed me the way Reed did last night, none of them. It frightens me how much he consumed me, how much he gave me exactly what I wanted. How he knew exactly what I needed with the answer to the only question he asked me. I wonder if it's like that with all his women; I wonder if he had it with Lacey, but as I've proven, I'm way too much of a chicken shit to sit around and find out. Facing him this morning is too hard; it will bring forth feelings I don't want to talk about. Not right now, not when I'm as raw emotionally as I am right now. I'm still trying to get over Justin yelling at me.

I quickly put clothes on and make my way out of his house, locking up. I feel like shit, sneaking out the way I am, but I can't face him this morning. I can't open myself up that way and let him see what's inside my heart. It's too soon. I'm running because I'm scared of how intense it was, and I'm trying to convince myself the connection I know was there–wasn't.

My only concern is getting to my car and getting the hell out of Dodge. It's self-preservation, and I'm feeling it big time. As I pull onto the highway, I grab my cell phone and dial the only good girlfriend I have. Morgan and I don't talk about private things often, usually because I'm scared she's going to tell Justin what I have going on in my private life, but she's always been there for me. The fact that she'll soon be my sister-in-law, because Justin finally pulled his head out of his ass, doesn't change how much I need her. I only hope she can keep my confidence, if even for a little while. When I need to bitch like a woman, she's always got my back, and right now I need a woman's perspective in a bad way.

"Hey, chick," she answers on the first ring. "What's goin' on?"

I can't even get the words out before the sob escapes my chest. It's so unexpected I pull off the road and park my car, letting the emotion overtake me. It feels good to let it out because it's so overwhelming.

"Sass, what's wrong?" she asks, concern in her voice. "Do I need to come get you? You're scaring me."

"I'm sorry." I sniffle. "I don't even know where this is coming from." I'm fighting embarrassment at the way I'm acting.

Her voice is soft. "Why don't you tell me what happened? It's the best place to start," she nudges me gently.

It's always been this way with her. She's always known me better than I know myself, and it's refreshing to have someone like that in my life when Justin presses all the time. She directs and genuinely cares about my feelings.

"I slept with Reed last night. Twice." There's no shame in my voice. I'm not ashamed of it, but I'm assuming it meant nothing to him. And since I didn't stick around to find out, it's tearing my heart apart. It's an ache I hadn't counted on, a knife twisting painfully.

"Oohhh, honey," she answers. "Let me guess, this wasn't part of the whole 'pretend to be together' plan?"

I shake my head and then realize she can't see me. "It wasn't in mine, and I'm almost positive it wasn't in his. We both had a bad day yesterday, and one thing lead to another, and it kind of happened the first time. The second time I think it happened because we both wanted it. Neither one of us realized the first time would be so good."

"This is something you've wanted for years, Sass. Explain to me what's wrong with this situation."

I'm trying to figure out why this bothers me so much. I'm not entirely sure, but I'm panicked in a way I never have been before. "Because it meant too much to me," I admit. "I don't think it meant much to Reed. I'm positive he was happy to get off."

There it is. What I'm afraid of, and I want to smack my own head because I knew this was inevitable with this stupid plan we've come up with.

Morgan is quiet on the other end of the line. "Why don't you not jump to conclusions? Why don't you ask him?"

"And then make things awkward when I confess things about myself that only you know? No thank you. He doesn't need me to confirm I've harbored this crush since I was a kid," I yell, biting my thumbnail as I realize I've seriously fucked myself over.

"Then what are you going to do? Pretend like nothing happened?" she asks, and I can tell by her tone of voice she thinks it's a horrible idea.

I'm trying to figure this out, really trying to figure it out. I've gotten myself into a situation that's going to be a bitch to get out of. It's of my own doing, and that's what hurts the most—the fact I have completely done this to myself. What kind of an idiot am I?

"Maybe it's time we stage our break up?"

Morgan snorts. "You've only been together a few days."

"So we tried it and it didn't work. We're just better as

friends," I defend my decision. People would believe that, right? Or maybe we can blame it on Justin. Right now, my brother is on my shit list, and he can take the blame for everything in my life.

"You keep tellin' yourself that, Sass, but anyone who's seen the two of you together knows there's no way the two of you are only friends." Her voice is quiet as she finishes her thought. "I wish the two of you could see what everyone else sees. What we've all been seeing for years."

I don't know what she means, and I'm not sure I really do want to know. It's a loaded statement, and to be honest, I've had enough revelations for the day. This one is better left untouched.

"I'm gonna think about it." It's the closest thing to a prom- ise I can make. "I'll figure out what to do, and it'll be all good."

The problem? Her sigh says she doesn't believe it, and I know deep in my heart I don't believe it.

When did all of this become so complicated? I know with clarity it was the moment I agreed to this stunt. I had hoped to keep my heart out of it, but I know now it was stupid to even consider it.

When this is over, my heart will not be broken—it'll be completely shattered.

CHAPTER THIRTEEN

Reed

IT'S ANOTHER HOT day in Alabama, and I should be in the best mood ever after what happened with Sass last night, but I'm not. Right now I'm in a foul mood—again—because she skipped out on me this morning. I've escaped to my office so I'm not in danger of injuring myself on the job site. I can't figure it out; I thought she was into it. The way she came on my cock told me she was into it, but this morning, she was gone. Not just gone in the fact she was in the shower while I was in bed. No, she was gone without a trace. I've called her, and the call's gone straight to voicemail. Even that's pissing me off.

"You need to check on those applicants who have applied for the new positions we put the ads in the paper for," my secretary, Alexa, is telling me.

I nod, but I'm not really listening to her. She's been with me since I started the company. She'd been a single mom who needed a job; I was a young guy who needed someone cheap. In the early years, she brought her kids to the office, and I paid her minimum wage. Luckily for both of us, we've been around to see each other grow.

"Are you listening to me?" she asks as she slams the folder down on the desk hard enough to get my attention.

"Applicants. I need to look at them," I bite off in a voice

that tells her not to fuck with me. Again, we've worked together long enough we know when to leave each other alone.

"I'll grab the applications I've weeded out and put them on your desk." She eyes me. "In the meantime, Justin pulled up. Maybe you should go talk to your best friend about what's crawled up your ass."

I groan in frustration. Justin is not who I want to see, but this has been brewing for a while, and I know it. Rolling my head, I let out a deep sigh as I walk through the front door of my office and catch Justin right as he's getting out of his truck. "Long time no see," I tell him, hoping that's a good place to open up dialogue.

"It's been a minute." He holds his hand out to mine for a handshake.

When I grasp it, I know it's the wrong thing to do. He pulls me towards him and lays a right hook into my jaw. I shake my head, moving my jaw, making sure it's not broken. Not even going to lie; I'm seeing stars. "I deserved that." I wince. Especially after last night, and I know without a doubt he doesn't know about that yet. It's too early. His ass probably hasn't even made it into the office yet. He goes to job sites first, not dragging ass into the office until after two usually.

Getting my footing back, I deliver him a hook of my own. "That's for makin' her cry yesterday."

We're quiet for a few minutes, both of us trying to get our bearings, Justin trying to staunch the flow at his eyebrow. "Did you have to aim for my fuckin' eyebrow? What if I need stiches?" he asks as he uses the edge of his shirt while looking into his truck's side-view mirror.

"I can't help it that you're shorter than me. That's where it's most comfortable for me to swing," I defend from where I sit on the bed of his pickup, willing my jaw to stop aching.

Eventually he comes back and sits on the tailgate next to me. We're silent for what seems like a long time.

"She's my sister, Reed, and it pisses me off; you're using her."

Those are the words I've waited to hear from him, and I wonder if I can be honest with him. "I don't know what to say to you."

"I know." Justin nods. "You've treated me differently since all the shit went down with Taylor, but you gotta know, dude. I ain't jealous of you or anything you've got. If nothing else, I know if you *really* care about Sass, she's gonna be well taken care of."

I sigh as I lean my head back. Two weeks after I found Lacey and Taylor, I confronted Taylor, and it was the worst conversation of my life. I'd be lying if I wasn't honest and admit it had changed my relationship with Justin, but only because I didn't want the same thing to happen with him.

"Why?" I ask, my voice hoarse as I confront the man I once called one of my best friends.

The smile on his face is slimy, and for the first time, I realize what a cold, calculating bastard this guy can be. I've known for a little while something's been off with him, but this wasn't what I expected at all.

"You've got it all, Golden Boy Reed. You were the captain of the football team, king of our Senior Prom, you've always gotten the girl, and everything you touch works. That loan you took out for RS Construction? Never in your wildest dreams should you have been able to pay that fucker off. Justin and I? We've struggled trying to pay ours back. You've thrived, and while Justin's not jealous of you, fuck if I am. I want what you got, Reed, so I started with your girl."

I can't believe what I'm hearing, and I'll be damned if this little shit gets anything of mine. Gone is the cross promotion I've used with his body shop, gone is my fucking good word. I won't badmouth him, but I sure as fuck won't try to help him out ever again.

"How did you do it, Taylor?" *Because I want to know. I want to know how five years went down the drain. What does he have that I don't?*

Taylor gives me the same cold grin. "Time, my brother."

"I ain't your fuckin' brother." *I shove him back against the wall of his body shop.* "Nobody will ever mistake us for that again, believe that shit."

"Lacey is the type of woman who needs time. She needs to know she's important and you won't call off a night of sex because you've worked hard on a job site or maybe you gotta work late. She needs the dick, my man, and I was there to give it to her."

The anger coursing through my body is palpable. I don't know if he realizes how close I am to killing him with a single blow to the head.

"She's a party girl, you know that."

"Yeah, I know she's always been the type of girl who likes to go out and have a good time." *I don't understand why we're talking about this.*

"You're not getting it. She likes to party, you know? Do a little blow once in a while. She craves it a little now." *Taylor winks at me.*

Blow? "You're doin' drugs?"

"Not everybody is a boy scout like you. There's a lot you don't know about your best friend, Reed. If you only knew the shit I've pulled under your nose over the years."

That's it, I can't wait anymore. There's a reason Taylor never started on the football team or went all-state like Justin and I did. He wasn't committed to the weight room. I reach back, and with all the anger I have in my body, I hit him. The sound is sickening, and he falls in a heap on the floor. Knocked the fuck out.

I use my boot to kick his foot, all too aware he's not moving. I reach into his pants pocket and pull his cell phone out, searching for Lacey's number. It's long since gone from my own cell phone. I take a picture of her boy toy and text her, letting her know what dick has just knocked hers out.

I throw the cell phone down and walk out.

I hadn't realized until this moment how much that had affected my relationship with Justin, but he's right, it has.

"I haven't meant for it to affect us, but hearing those words he said, knowing I'd spent so much of my life looking out for him and having him repay me like that," I run my hand through my hair, "it fucked me up."

Justin takes a deep breath. "It would anybody, but I'm tellin' you, I'm gonna be here for you, no matter what happens, unless you fuck Sass over." He shoots me a glare. "I don't know what's going on between the two of you, but I suggest you figure it out, because I know both of you. Neither of you do shit half-assed, and this had bad idea written on it from the get-go, but the crazy thing is, I've never seen either one of you so happy. If this is what it takes, then this is what it takes, but I won't be put in the middle if it goes south."

"Understood."

"Good." He nods. "Now let's do something neither of us have ever done before. Let's go have a beer in the middle of a work day. Given the fact I have a shiner, you've got a bruise on your jaw, and both of our knuckles are cut up, I think we deserve it."

An idea has never held as much appeal to me as this one does. "Let's go." I laugh as I hop off the tailgate and go to the passenger side.

"Wait, I'm drivin'?"

I climb up into the truck. "Your idea. If we get too drunk, Morgan can drive us home."

I'm not sure Sass wants to see me today, so I don't mention her name. For the first time in a year, it seems like life is finally getting back to normal.

CHAPTER FOURTEEN

Reed

THREE DAYS. THREE really long days. Sass has ignored my attempts to contact her for that long, and I can't understand it. I thought she had a good time the other night. Sure, I hadn't planned on us having sex, and I'm almost positive she didn't either, but I can't figure out why she's gone dark on me. From the way she was moaning and thrusting, I know it wasn't me being bad in the sack. Doing it the second time was even better than the first, and I can't figure out what the fuck I've done wrong.

She won't even return my calls when I leave nice, sweet voicemails. Or when I tell her Justin and I have come to agreement, we fought it out and drank it out, and now we're good.

Grabbing my phone out of my jeans pocket, this time I try a text.

How's it going? I hope you're doing okay after the other night.
I'd like to do it again.

I contemplate adding a smiley face, but that seems like a douche move. The whole text idea seems like a douche move, but I send it anyway and hope she doesn't take it as me trying to solicit her. It makes it sound almost as if all I want from her is sex, and I hate that, but we're at this fucking awkward stage, and we have to get past it. I should have clarified I liked it all. The company, the dinner, the companionship, and yes, the sex, but it all felt good.

"Boss, someone's here to see you."

I'm in the office again today, signing off on a bunch of invoices and orders my secretary has been bitching about me signing for weeks. This is tedious, and I fucking hate it, so I welcome the distraction.

"Yeah, I'm free." I have no idea who might be here to see me, but if it means not having to do this paperwork, it could be the sheriff and I'd be happy.

The air sucks from the room when I notice Sass standing in the doorway.

"Hey." She smiles softly at me. She's carrying a folder in her hands, and I struggle with the need to scream at her. Ask her where the fuck she's been for three days. Ask her why she hasn't returned my calls, why she's been ignoring me. It makes me angry, but I'm trying like hell to keep my temper in check, to keep in control.

"Hey yourself." I hold up my cell phone. "I've been trying to get hold of you. In fact I just sent you a text."

"Yeah." She licks her lips as she has a seat from across me, putting the folder on my desk. "About that." She sighs. "Things have been a little crazy."

I reach for the folder. "Obviously you're here on both business and personal, so let's get the business outta the way first. Then we can get to the personal. You're not running away again without the personal being discussed."

She nods and crosses her legs. I can see an expanse of tanned skin, and I want nothing more than to walk over to the other side of my desk and get all up in that skin. Instead I shake my head and try to pay attention to what she's telling me.

"Those are the purchase orders for the three homes you've contracted for with Justin. We need your signature to confirm." The way she talks is so controlled, and the polite way with which she conducts business transactions pisses me off immediately.

I know this; I've done this with him a million times. Our businesses are entwined together. Her attitude rubs salt in a wound I didn't know was there. It feels like it did with Lacey, when I realized all she cared about was the money, the fact I'm a respected businessman, and being on my arm. This hurts ten times more, and makes me a hundred times more pissed.

I angrily open the folder, scribble my signature on the contracts, and close it with a flourish.

"Now onto the personal."

Her eyes flash at me and her face flushes. "Reed, I...your face looks just as bad as Justin's," she finishes lamely.

I talk about what's really going on here, because it's obvious she doesn't want to. I'm not the kind of guy who can bury my head in the sand and hope things go away. I'm a man of action, and I want to know what the fuck happened. "Why were you not there when I woke up in the morning?" It's the question I've asked myself over and over again. Why did she leave?

She's quiet, and I know at this point I have to push her. She's withdrawing into herself, and I have to make her speak. If I don't, we're going to get nowhere. She may hate me for this, but I need answers. I need her to talk, and I need her to fight for this.

"I woke up hard as a rock, looking for you." My voice is dark with desire, even I can hear it. "Imagine my surprise when I realized you were gone."

"I can't do this," she blurts out, getting up, heading for the door. "We moved too fast. This is all too much, and I can't do it."

Confusion swirls in my head, because she was all on board

with this the other night, and I have to wonder what's changed. What's got her running scared? This isn't the Sass I've always known. "What's going on, Sass? And I want the fuckin' truth."

Tears are bright in her eyes as she turns back to look at me. "I think we should stage a breakup. I can't keep doing this. Reed, you're a hard guy to keep up with, and I don't think I'm the person to help you do this."

It's a bullshit excuse, and even I know that, but looking at her, she's devastated. I'm a bastard, but I'll use anything to help me get to the bottom of this. "You promised to help me," I accuse. "Lacey ripped my fucking heart out, and you promised."

She turns away from me. "I know. I know I did, but there's so much going on right now."

"Tell me how to fix it," I beg her. As crazy as this seems, I can't let two women walk away from me. This one is becoming a fixture in my thoughts, and I like having her around my house. I don't want to let her go. She's wormed herself into my life, like Justin warned me she would. I look forward to seeing her, talking to her, eating dinner with her.

She bites her lip. "I don't think you can, but please, give it some thought, Reed. Let me know what you want to do. I'll let you call the shots because I did offer this, it was my idea, but I want you to think it through clearly. Examine all sides and all scenarios."

She's serious. The question, the quiet devastation this might be over, is there in her eyes. "I'll think about it and get back to you."

"That's all I can ask." She turns the doorknob and smiles sadly at me as she walks out of my office.

I can't help but think my future just walked out the door, and damn if I don't know what to do about it.

CHAPTER FIFTEEN

Reed

I'M SURPRISED AT what Sass has suggested. I never expected those words to come out of her mouth, never expected her to be the one to have second thoughts or call this off. It's affected me in a way I wasn't prepared for. At the same time, I think I'm also shocked at the way the words have affected me. I thought when it was time for us to break up it would be something I'd be able to do easily. I'd be able to go on with my life and it not hurt, but fuck if hearing those words come from her mouth didn't hurt. It's a truth I've not been prepared for.

I've been happy with her, I realize. She's brought a happiness to my life I haven't had since the early days of my relationship with Lacey. Looking back on it now, I realize Lacey and I were toxic for one another. Not in the beginning, but definitely towards the end. I can see instances of where I should have known she was cheating on me, but I chose to ignore it. I chose to believe no matter what, we were together and we were happy. Little did I know I had been ignoring my own happiness. The weeks have taught me sometimes we settle. I'm not settling again, and I'm not ignoring this situation or letting Sass call the shots here. I'm not that kind of a man anymore.

Taking a deep breath, I park my truck in Justin's driveway. I called him earlier and told him I needed to talk, but I didn't tell him what about. I'm telling my best friend I've slept with his little sister and now she wants me out of her life. That's never easy.

"Hey, man," he yells from his front porch, beer in hand.

He's holding another one up towards me in greeting. I gratefully accept it and twist the top off with my bare hand. I'm going to need the alcohol to be honest, so I quickly take a long drink, relishing the coolness as it flows down my throat.

"What's going on?" he asks.

He's known me long enough to know I don't do heart-to-heart very often, and if I've asked to talk to him, it's serious. "Can we go out back?"

His backyard is incredible, almost like a rain forest, and instead of a pool, it's got a koi pond. I find Justin is more relaxed when he's out there, and I want him to be—relaxed as fuck. I don't want to fight my best friend tonight.

His eyebrows rise as he looks at me, question in his eyes. "Sure, if that's what you wanna do."

"NOT THAT I'M not happy to see you in a capacity that's not work related, and I'm happy we aren't beating the shit out of each other, but you're startin' to scare me, dude," Justin says as he glances at me.

We've been sitting on his deck for fifteen minutes, and I haven't said anything yet. Not because I don't have words to speak, but because I'm nervous as fuck. I clear my throat. "Just getting my thoughts together."

He turns to face me, handing me another beer because I'm done with the first one. His eyebrows rise, and I know, all of a sudden, he knows. "Does this have anything to do with Sass?"

I want to tell him no, but I've never been a liar, even when it would make things easier. "It does."

He sets his beer down. "Okay, I'm gonna do my best to remember you're my best friend in this world. I'm going to do my best to remember you've been there for me when other people weren't. You were there when my dad died, and you've always been there for her too. The other day, though, I knew something was going on. She was upset the other day, and I asked her if it had to do with you—she wouldn't say. My advice to you is be fucking honest with me. I need you to be honest with me. We've both gotten our licks in, and I don't want to have to hit you again."

This is the hardest thing I've ever had to do—to be honest with him in a way that makes me vulnerable. We've been best friends for years, but normally we do this shit together. One of us doesn't normally have to confess to the other. I figure it's like anything else—rip it off quick and deal with the consequences later.

My voice is low but determined. I won't be sorry we did this, I'll be sorry I'm going to disappoint my friend. "She and I slept together."

"Goddammit, Reed." My confession seems to unleash an anger in Justin I've seen before but never been on the receiving end of. "I trusted you, dude, trusted you with her. I assumed you wouldn't be the asshole who would break her heart. What the ever-loving fuck?"

"It just happened." The excuse sounds pitiful even to my own ears, like a fucking cop-out. It was so much more than "just happening", and I know, but I can't tell him. He doesn't see her like I do.

The look he gives me makes me want to bury myself under a mound of dirt. His eyes flash angrily at me, and I would do anything not to be the person putting this look on his face.

"Don't," he spits out. "Don't think I'm a fucking idiot. I know you. That sort of shit doesn't just *happen* with you." He shakes his head and lowers his voice. "Do you even care about her?"

Killing time, I take another drink from my beer and tilt my head back, looking up at the sky. "That's the bitch of this whole situation, I do. I want it to turn into something real, and damn if I know Sass wants it too, but she's scared. She wants to stage a break up."

"She's had a crush on you for years, Reed. Surely you knew. Hell, I know you knew."

"I did and I didn't." I shake my head. "I could see it sometimes, but there were other times I talked myself out of it. I told myself she looked at me like another brother, so I can understand why she's hesitant, but I know there was heat between us when we were together. You can't fake or manipulate that level of intensity or passion. That shit was real; I'm talking burn in my soul and tell our grandchildren about it in fifty years."

Justin breathes deeply through his nose and levels me with a stare. "Look, I can't say I'm not pissed about how some of this has worked out, but you're my best friend and she's my sister. I want the best for both of you, and if that's each other, then so be it. What I can tell you is when Sass has something in her head; you're fucked trying to convince her to change that idea."

I laugh because I know he's right. Stubborn is not even the word to describe Cassandra Straight when she gets an idea in her head. "You've got that shit right."

He lifts his beer up in salute, a wry smile on his face. "My thoughts and prayers are with you, my brother."

Good, I know I'm going to need them.

CHAPTER SIXTEEN

Sass

I CROSS MY legs under the desk and wince at the soreness between my thighs. I don't know what kind of voodoo magic Reed put on me when we slept together—or rather, fucked like bunnies—but days later I'm still feeling it. I hadn't thought it'd been that long, but maybe I was wrong. Maybe he was bigger than I thought he was. Either way, there's never been a man who's done it for me. Truthfully, I like sex, but with the men I've been with, I've rarely been truly satisfied. I have a sneaky suspicion that's one more thing Reed Shamrock has ruined for me.

If there was any way in this world I thought the two of us could be together without imploding, I would jump at the chance, but the fact of the matter is, it scares the shit out of me. Literally scares me.

So many questions come to mind, and they invade my thoughts at every hour of the day. What if we don't work out? What if we do work out? What does this mean for his friendship with Justin? Who will he spend holidays with? What does it mean for me and my own heart? It's a shitty situation to be in.

Reed hardly ever talks about his lack of family; that's why he's so close to us. If we don't work out, I don't want to remove the only family he's truly known from his life. That would kill me—if the broken heart didn't kill me first. It's not like he doesn't have family, but his parents were workaholics who never should have had a child. They believed in doing for themselves, and since he didn't go to college after high school, it was up to him to make his own way. The only thing Reed loved was carpentry, so RS Construction was born.

Too bad his success didn't help his relationship with his parents, and to this day, they still don't really talk. There's just no communication or feeling there. I don't want to be the next person in his life he doesn't communicate with.

"C'mon, Justin." I sigh. Waiting on him has become a huge part of my job. He runs later and later every day, and I know at some point we're going to have to have a talk about him respecting my time boundaries. That will be oh so pleasant.

I glance up at the clock and realize he's probably at least an hour out. I've done all the invoices for the day, scheduled appointments for the next day; frankly I have nothing else to do that's pressing. Booting up the computer, I log onto Facebook and decide to look around.

Reed and I are Facebook friends, so I click on his name and go in search of his pictures. For some reason, I'm nosey and want to snoop his old pics. There's a part of me that needs to see if he still has pics of him and Lacey up. Trust me, I know this is a stupid idea. It doesn't have a good ending, but I'm a glutton for punishment, and I want to compare the way he looks at her to the way he looks at me.

And there they are. I can't help clicking on one of them. He's looking at her like she's the most amazing person in the world. God, what I wouldn't give for him to look at me like that. I realize, even as I'm thinking all of this, I'm hoping for something I'm not allowing to happen. I'm the one putting a stop to these feelings developing, I'm the one who doesn't want to give them the time to grow, yet I'm blaming it on Reed.

As I'm surfing and snooping, a message bubble pops up, and I see Lacey's name. She's sent me a PM; she hasn't done that in a long time. Curiosity gets the best of me, and I click on it.

"Hey girl, I hope you and Reed are doing well. I saw your car there overnight a few days ago. Just letting you know not to get too comfortable in my kitchen or my old house. I can have it back whenever I want it. Reed is putty in my hands, and all you are right now is a distraction from what he lost. Keep that in mind, sweets. xoxo"

That straight up pisses me off in ways I can't even begin to explain. How dare this bitch? For one thing, I'm super competitive; for another, she gave him up, not the other way around. For a third, how could you see Reed's cock and want someone else's? None of it makes sense to me.

Fury building in my gut, I have my hands poised on the keyboard, ready to respond to her, to really lay into her as only I know I can, when the door to the office opens and the man she's talking about appears. He looks sheepish and like he's had a rough couple of days. There are dark circles under his eyes, his hair is unkept, as if he's been running his hands through it, and his beard is at least a few days old. It's desperately in need of a trim. For the longest time we don't talk, but I can't seem to make my mouth move. What if he's here to tell me my idea of ending this is a good one? The fear of him telling me that is what makes me want to fight for it.

I have been such a damn idiot—scared of everything with this man—and it's going to come back and bite me in the ass.

"Hey," he finally says, the corner of his mouth lifting up in the cutest smile I've ever seen. It melts my heart and makes my pulse race in a way I can't even describe. My heart flutters like it used to when I'd catch a glimpse of him sitting in our living room watching TV with Justin and Taylor. It was the forbidden, and now it kind of feels the exact same way again.

I can't help but smile back. "Hey."

He shifts his weight on his legs and sticks his hands in his pockets. "You mind if we talk?" He's the one holding out a peace offering; he's swallowed his pride and come to me. It's something I hadn't thought he would do, but if he's willing to extend the olive branch, then I'm grabbing hold of it and not letting go.

I might regret this with everything I am, but I answer anyway. I need to know the answers, I need us to talk about this, and I need to stop living my life in fear. "Come on in and have a seat, I think it's time we have a serious conversation."

And I'm scared to death of how we'll leave this room.

CHAPTER SEVENTEEN

Reed

S ASS PUTS ON a good show; she always has. It doesn't matter what it is she's facing, she always does it in this stoic way she has. I think she'd rather die than let someone know they've hurt or disappointed her. For most everyone, they can't see it, but me, I do, and I don't want this sitting here between us. I don't want the show either. I want the real Sass, the one who has feelings. The one I can touch, the one who's hiding right there beneath the surface. This is me, for fuck's sake, not some asshole off the street.

"What did you want to talk about?" she asks, moving stuff around on her desk so she doesn't have to look at me.

I don't know if she's doing it for my benefit or hers, but she can't seem to meet my eyes. That's frightening to me and for the possible saving of our relationship. I need her to be honest with me, and I need to know how she's feeling. The only way I can do it is if I'm looking at her. She can lie all she wants, but her face and eyes never lie. They are the window to everything that is Sass.

"Our agreement. The one where you agreed to help me piss Lacey off, it's not exactly working for me anymore." I figure those words will get her attention, and when her head snaps up, I know they've done exactly what I wanted them to.

She opens her mouth to speak, but I hold up my hand to shush her. "Not in the way you think. Hear me out, Sass. Give me a few minutes, and just listen. Don't let your brain overthink what I'm saying. All I'm asking for is a chance to talk to you."

"Okay, but I still think we should end this. You know my feelings." She says it in this smart-ass, sassy way she's had since she was a kid. I hate the tone of voice, and I hate the look on her face when she does it.

I'm pissed. I know the look on my face is fucking stormy. "I do know your feelings—the real ones, not the bullshit line you're feeding me. The way your pussy gripped my cock when I was all up inside you?" I lean my head to the side and tilt my mouth in a smart ass grin. "You can't fake that, baby doll."

Her face flushes, and I know I've hit a nerve with her. Good, I want to hit a nerve; I want her to realize how bull-headed and stubborn she's being.

"I don't think we should end this. The other night…" I run my hand through my hair and shake my head because I can't comprehend what we shared. It was intense. "Was so fucking amazing, I wasn't prepared for it, Sass. I didn't know the two of us together would be like that." My voice is hoarse as I hit her with some realness I hadn't been prepared to face myself, but if I'm going to convince her we belong together, I need to be honest with myself as well as her.

"I didn't either," she admits, biting her bottom lip, her eyes taking on a faraway look. Hopefully she's remembering how good the sex was between us. The way I made her scream, she made me moan, and how it felt when I held her in my arms. It was right. "It was intense."

"It was," I agree, my heart soaring as I realize she might be seeing this the way I do. Maybe for once we're both on the same damn page. "And I kind of want to see where it goes. When we started this, there was no way I'd want to put myself out there, ever again, but Sass, you make me laugh and smile. That's something neither one of us can fake."

I hope I'm breaking that barrier, hope I'm making sense to her. I'm pleading my case in a way that's going to make her see there is a shot for this to work. I'm older than her; I know this shit doesn't come along every day. I took it for granted before; I'm not taking it for granted again. You're given a shot at it more than once, and you grab it by the ass and you don't let it go. The second time you fuck it into submission. "Let's see where this can go."

She shifts in her seat. "My only problem is Lacey." Her lips are together in a firm line, and my heart sinks.

"She's not even a part of my life anymore," I argue, hoping she believes me. Lacey seems to be a non-negotiable topic for her, and I don't want my ex-fiancée to cause any more problems between us. Taylor showed me exactly who the woman is I thought I was going to marry, and she's not the type of person I want or need in my life.

Turning the computer screen towards me, she shows me the message Lacey sent a few seconds ago according to the timestamp.

"I don't do well sharing, Reed. You know that."

I do. I can remember once when she was a little kid, I grabbed a chicken nugget off her plate and ended up singing soprano for a couple of days after. "There's no sharing," I assure her. "I'm not taking her back."

"You were going to marry her," she reminds me. Her voice is pained, like those words are hard to push past her throat. I guess it does, since she's harbored a crush on me for all these years. The same way it hurts me to think tomorrow she could be gone if I fuck this up.

"Until she ruined it all by lying to me. In no universe, alternate or otherwise, will I ever trust her again."

I can see her mulling it around in her head, and I wonder if I've gotten to her. "What do you say, Sass? Wanna try this out for real and see what happens?"

I watch as a smile spreads across her face and she gives me a wink. "Why the hell not? I haven't had any better offers."

Throwing my head back, I laugh like I haven't laughed in a long time. "Then let me tell you, this offer is on the table and it's negotiable, but I really hope you'll see things my way. Do you accept?"

She gets up and walks around the desk, my eyes following along. I'm waiting for her to accept, waiting for her to give us a chance. The tension is thick, I'm worried she's going to say forget it and move the fuck on. I offer my hands to her, and she reaches down and grabs them, pulling me up so I'm standing in front of her. Circling her arms around my waist, she snuggles in for a hug, and I wrap my arms tightly around her.

The "I accept" is muffled against my chest, but two words have never been clearer or meant more to me in my life.

CHAPTER EIGHTEEN

Sass

GOOD IDEAS ARE always good in theory, and sometimes they can backfire and leave everyone involved a hot smoking mess. I'm hoping and praying sticking to this relationship is in fact one of those good ideas. Since Reed and I talked a few days ago about what we both want, we've had a couple of phone conversations and we've texted a lot. Yesterday he mentioned to me he didn't have anything going on today, and I thought maybe we should hang out together. Weekends are days couples normally spend with one another. The only problem is I haven't shared this with him; I want it to be a surprise.

This is the first time I've ever showed up at his house unannounced, and to say I'm nervous is a huge understatement. This is what girlfriends do, and we definitely haven't put that kind of label on what this is between us yet. That doesn't stop me, though. If I want to make this work, I have to find a way to make it do just that. Sitting around waiting on something to happen doesn't mean it's going to. Action will do that, and action is what it will take. If I have to take action, then so be it; it's time for me to take my life and my future into my own hands.

Knocking, I hold my breath as I wait for him to answer the door. My heart pounds and my palms sweat as I realize exactly what I'm doing. I'm putting myself out there in a huge way with this idea I have, and I really hope it works out. I haven't given much thought to what will happen if it doesn't work out. I only know I have to give this a shot. My brain doesn't want to come up with those scenarios, because I know they will kill any chance at happiness if I think of them. For this to work, I have to try. I have to give it my all and make Reed want to give it his too.

The door opens, and the surprised look on his face is replaced with one of happiness as he sees it's me. "Sass?"

Judging by the way he's dressed, he'd planned to spend the day in the house, lounging on the couch. The pajama pants look cute though, and the fact he's not wearing a shirt is even better. I give him a small smile and hope like hell I'm cute enough to make him want to spend the day with me.

Reed

TO SAY I'M surprised at Sass' visit is an understatement, but it's not a bad surprise at all. I had been sitting in my living room, wondering what the fuck Sass was doing, because I wanted to see her, but I didn't want to monopolize her time. We had never discussed how weekends would be spent, and I wasn't sure how to approach the topic, but now she's come to me.

I reach out and pull her towards me. She looks like the Sass I've always known, but now I know what's under the clothes she's wearing, and I can't help the reaction my body has as she easily comes into my arms. It feels like we're sharing a secret no one else is privy too. This feeling is nice, and I want more of it.

"What are you doing here?" I ask as I run my hands down the tank top covering her torso to the frayed denim of the cut-off shorts that hug her ass in a way I can't wait to see. My hands cup the edges, and settle her against me as I pull my face back so I can see hers.

Her face is flushed as she reaches up and kisses me along my jawline. No woman has ever kissed me there before, but this is the second or third time she's done it, and it gets me hot in a way I can't even describe. It's such a trusting gesture. The softness of her lips against the harshness of my skin.

She pulls away enough to separate us, but my hands grip her hips tightly. "We haven't really dated so much, ya know? I figured it'd be a good idea if we do something we both enjoy," she explains.

Immediately my mind goes back to the one night she's spent here with me. I can think of a few things we do very well, but I get what she means. "Alright, you got me, what are we doing?"

"When was the last time you went fishing at the pond you put in?" she asks, almost shyly. Her eyes focus on my lips, and I think it's because she doesn't want to look at me. I'm not used to this shy Sass, but I have to admit, it makes me want to give her everything she wants.

"This is the life." I cast my line and bury the edge of the fishing pole into the wet dirt. Grabbing a beer from the Yeti we've brought with us, I toss it over to him as I take my own out.

Justin's stretched out in a lawn chair across from me, hat pulled down low over his eyes. He pops open the top on the can of beer and takes a healthy drink from it. "You're damn right. This has been the longest week of my life."

I know how he feels. Sometimes running your own business is worse than working for someone else. "Right? Everything that could go wrong went wrong this week."

"According to old Nell down at the diner, mercury is in retrograde or some shit. All's I know is I've had to replace two mowers, the starter on my truck, and Morgan's garbage disposal went out."

I look over at him. "You fixed the garbage disposal?" Plumbing and pipes is usually not Justin's specialty.

"Fuck no, I need you to go over there and fix it for her," he fires back.

I shake my head. If this isn't what friends are for, I don't know what is. When I'm finally comfortable, my cell phone beeps with a text message, and when I look at it, I know this day is over. Lacey hadn't wanted me to come in the first place, and I should have known she'd do something to fuck it up.

"Once." I snort. "With Justin. It wasn't even for an hour; I got called back to the house." I don't want to mention Lacey's name, but she hated that pond, she hated the time I spent with friends, and now I'm a year away from the relationship, I can see it. She was a virus that sucked the life out of my friendships, and I'm pissed I wasn't able to see it back when I was in it.

"Think you want to do that today?" she asks, biting her bottom lip as she looks up at me.

There's question in her eyes, and an uncertainty. I know Sass, and I know this is a big thing for her to ask me. Fishing was a past time she, Justin, and her dad had done together before her dad got sick and passed away. Knowing she wants me to do this with her is huge. It's a vulnerability for her, and there's no way in hell I'm going to say no.

"Let me go change." I indicate the pajama pants I'm still wearing. "We'll take the four wheeler down." The road to get there is pretty rough, and I don't want to mess up her car or get my truck dirty.

Her eyes brighten, and it makes me feel like I've handed her the most precious gift ever. She's easy to please, easy to make happy, and I'm not used to it, but I sure as hell want to continue to put the smile on her face.

CHAPTER NINETEEN

Sass

I HOLD TIGHTLY onto Reed's waist as he navigates the rutted road leading to the pond. I'm purposely all up on him, letting the front of me touch every back part of him. He's changed into an old football shirt with the sleeves cut out, the arm holes hang down so low I can see the edges of his hips. I can see the tattoo he has on his rib cage every time the shirt moves, like it gives me a peep show, and I want to lick that ink with my tongue. Reed is a good ole boy, but on certain occasions he does like his rock music, and the tattoo is the result of a night he and Justin had after a *Disturbed* concert. I don't know the meaning of the tattoo or what lead up to it, but it's still hot to see on his body.

"Hang on," he yells over the noise of the four wheeler as we dip down into a part of the road that's partially covered by water. I push my aviators further up on my nose and do as he's instructed. My hands clasp over his abdomen, and I wonder what he will think if I were to move my hands down a few inches and cup him, but I can't bring myself to yet.

As we make our way up the hill on the other side, I recognize the green and blue colors of the pond, and it's as gorgeous as I remember it. It's a little windy today, so the water is rippling. There's a copse of trees on the east side, and I breathe a sigh of relief as he directs us over to that side. It's a hot, muggy one today, like every other Alabama summer day, and the protection the trees offer will be greatly appreciated.

"I can't believe you don't come out here more often," I scold him, taking a look around, taking it all in. This is something I want in my own home, this serenity. "It's so peaceful out here."

He shakes his head as he puts the stuff down, hands on his hips. "In the hustle and bustle of things, I forget it," he admits. "I'm glad I have you to remind me of it now." He leans down and gives me a kiss. It's not the heat of others we've shared; it's sweet, almost reverent. It's one of the first ones we've spontaneously had, and I tuck it away in my memory bank.

"I'm never gonna let you forget it," I tease him as I grab the poles and bait.

Reed

TWO HOURS LATER, we're lounging in chairs, and Sass gives me a bored, disbelieving look as she pushes her sunglasses down on her nose so her eyes are exposed to mine.

"Are you sure you put fish in this pond? Have you fed them? Have they died? Did they leave you for someone who actually cared? Two hours, Reed, and we haven't gotten a bite."

Her tone is accusing, and I can't help but laugh. "I hope they haven't died. I spent a shit ton stocking it, and yes, I do make sure they're fed. Maybe we're not casting in the right place," I defend myself. Cutting my eye towards her, I throw out another option. "Maybe our bait sucks."

She'd brought the bait, and I can see her get her back up.

"Chicken livers have never failed me before, thank you very fuckin' much. They are a family hand-me-down, tested, tried, and true for many generations."

"Well, honey, it seems like this is a first."

I don't see the handful of mud until it hits the side of my head. I'm shocked as I shake my head, trying to get it out of my hair. "Sass." My voice is a warning. "Did you mean to throw mud at me?"

She holds another handful. "Don't you ever talk bad about my decision to use chicken livers as bait." She smirks, taking aim again.

I'm quick as I leap from my chair and tackle her to the soft ground. She squeals as I push her further into the ground, getting both of us muddy. "I give!" she yells.

As we roll around, I laugh. It's been so long since I've been able to have fun with someone like this. It never even entered my mind with Lacey. She wasn't a fun girl, she took things way too seriously, and Sass is like a balm for my soul. I roll again so she's underneath me. "I think we should head back. If we let this mud dry, we'll never get it off." My mouth is inches away from hers. Her dark eyes look into my light ones, and she lifts her head to press her lips against mine. All too soon the kiss is over.

"You're right." She pushes against me so we can both stand.

As we pack up, I look over at her. "Sass?"

"Yeah?"

I give her my best grin, knowing my dimple shows. "Thank you for this."

She rewards me with a smile of her own. "No problem. Sometimes it's nice to have fun and not worry about anything else."

That's one thing I always knew about her and admired, but I'm learning the more time we spend together, she lives for the fun. As someone who spends much of his life being serious and taking care of other people, this is an area of my life I need help with, and I'm lucky she seems to be taking it upon herself to do just that.

Sass

THE HEAT OF the shower is engulfing both of us. I lean my head back as his fingers work my hair gently, getting out the mud that's already dried. I moan in pleasure as they massage my scalp.

"Reed." I gasp, letting my head fall forward, resting it on the wall of the shower.

It had been his idea to shower together, telling me I needed help getting the mud out of my hair. I could tell by the mischievous look in his eyes and the grin on his face he'd had other plans, but I hadn't minded one bit.

He leans forward, sucking on the sensitive skin of my neck he's exposed as he's worked my hair into a lather. "Your back is one of the sexiest things I've ever seen." He breathes in my ear. "And this ass." His hands slide down, cupping the globes.

The steam makes it seem we are some sort of dream state. I can't really see his face, because he's behind me. The heat of his breath on my shoulder and the indentions of his fingers as he digs them into the flesh of my backside are the only things I'm aware of. I push it out, giving him more to hold onto.

"Please, Reed, touch me where I need it," I beg him. We've been playing in this shower for a long time, and the ache I have between my legs is almost at critical.

He chuckles and moves one hand to the front of my body. My legs shake as he runs his fingers over my slit, moving down to push two inside me. I pant against the tile of the shower, thrusting my body back out at him. My fingers and nails are grabbing for an anchor that isn't there. I'm trying desperately to hold onto reality.

"Goddamn, Sass." Hot breath fans as his teeth nip my flesh. "So fucking tight."

I squeeze my muscles against his fingers again, but it's not enough. I need him inside me, I need him filling me. No other man I've ever been with has filled me the way he has. They've never made me this crazy, never worked me up so quickly. I throw my head back against his shoulder. "Fuck me, Reed. I need you to fuck me."

He growls and flips me around, lifting me up. There's a seat in the shower, and he moves us so he's sitting on it, grabbing me around the waist, situating my legs on either side of him.

"C'mon, Sass, I know how much you like to ride," he taunts me.

In one swift stroke, I take him, groaning as he goes deeper than I imagined he could. I tilt my head back, letting the water hit my face. It thrusts my tits out so Reed can capture one with his mouth. He worries the nub between his teeth, sucking tightly as I move up and down on his length. Every inch of him is hard against my softness, and I know he feels it too the way he's biting and sucking on me. His fingers are digging into my flesh, and the feelings coursing through my body make me moan loudly.

"That's right, Sass. Let me hear it. Show me what you want."

Grasping his shoulders, I use them for leverage, picking up my pace. My body is tightening, and I'm surprised, because never, since I began having sex, have I been able to get off this way. It's usually a longer process and involves me always coming after the man in my life.

I'm breathing heavily, panting really at this point. One of my hands leaves Reed's shoulder and grasps his hair, tightening, making sure he doesn't move his mouth from my nipple.

"Don't stop," I beg. "Keep biting, keep sucking, I'm almost there," I circle my hips around his, move up and down, keeping our rhythm consistent. "Please don't fucking stop."

And there it is, I fly. Somewhere as I'm riding out the waves of the feelings consuming my body, Reed breathes a sigh of relief, his body relaxes, his heat is deep inside me, and I know he's come too, but I can't bring myself to care.

He's ruined me for any other man—ever again.

CHAPTER TWENTY

Reed

W E'RE IN THE kitchen, sneaking glances at one another over plates of leftover pizza.

She's sitting on the counter, wearing one of my shirts, her wet hair curly down her back and over her shoulder. This is a way I haven't seen her yet, and it appeals to me. Lacey always had to be made up and look perfect. Sass isn't caught up in how she looks twenty-four hours of the day, and I love the laid-back look she's sporting right now. She's not embarrassed to be herself or let me see her looking anything less than perfect. It's refreshing, and I try not to get completely fucked up in the fact I think she's sexier this way than any other way I've seen her.

Standing in front of her, my eyes follow her tongue as it sneaks out and grabs a piece of cheese that's falling from the pizza and almost groan as I think about that same tongue on my cock. I stand in front of her, conscious of how small she is compared to me even sitting up on the counter. She stops eating and gives me a look. It's not a sultry one, but it's not accusatory either. It's one I've never seen before.

"Why do you keep that around?" She points her head to the island in the middle of the kitchen.

"Because it's handy to use when I bring groceries in and when I'm cooking."

She shakes her head. "No, I mean the countertop."

Suddenly it hits me, what she's saying. The countertop had been a point of contention for Lacey and me. Too big, too heavy, and way too fucking expensive, I'd argued. In the end, I'd had to build extra support in the floor, and then I'd had to do some free work in exchange for the price to be knocked down. Marble wasn't my thing, and it didn't match the granite in the rest of the kitchen. It was also a far cry away from the stone I had wanted to use to match the outside kitchen work. Another reminder to me that what I had wanted didn't really matter to her, had never really mattered to her. We'd fought over the monstrosity for days, and she'd even left the house, going to stay with her mom. Looking back now, that should have given me a clue as to how easy it would be for her to run from me. Too bad I hadn't taken it for what it was back then. Maybe I could have saved all of us some heartache.

"Never thought about it," I answer, because it's the truth. It wasn't even a blip on my radar until Sass opened her mouth. It doesn't make me sad anymore, it doesn't hurt to look at it anymore, but what it does do is make my skin itch to get rid of it.

All of a sudden, I can't stand looking at it, and I want it gone. I have the piece of stone out in the garage I had originally wanted to put there, and I realize now I can. This is my home, no one else's. If I want to do this, I can; if I want to walk around naked on my hands, I can do that too. There's no one here to tell me otherwise.

"You ever done demo?" I ask her, an idea forming in my head. If I'm going to do this, I want her to be a part of it too. She's one hundred percent the reason I'm doing as well as I am right now. I'm man enough to admit that. Sass is warming my heart and calming my soul more than I ever anticipated she would.

"Can't say I have." She takes another leisurely bite of her pizza, trying to hide a smile. I can see it though, curling up behind the food she's holding in front of her.

"You want to?" I want her to. I want her to be a part of this, to be my partner in crime. Like I want her to be my partner in life. That thought hits me across the chest so hard I almost have to take a step back. Is that really what I'm thinking right now, or is it because we've had such a great day together? I know I can't express to her what I'm thinking, I don't want to lead her on, but I know later I'll examine my thoughts and I'll get my head on completely straight.

She thinks about it for a minute before gifting me with a mischievous smile. "Does it mean I'll get to see you without a shirt on, hammering things?"

I walk over and grab her around the waist. "That's exactly what it means, and if you're good, I'll let you swing the hammer too."

She laughs, her eyes bright. "Sounds good to me. Let's get started."

Thirty minutes later, after we've laid plastic and I've gotten the sledgehammer out, I'm taking back a piece of my life when I strike that countertop. As it crumbles, I realize I'm the one who's going to pick up those pieces of my life and put them back together. I realize I'm strong enough to do it now. I wasn't in the beginning, and it's okay to admit, but now, I can do this. I've got this, as long as I have Sass by my side.

Lacey no longer has a hold over me, and getting rid of this piece of shit countertop feels a million times better than it should.

"You want to do it?" I ask her, holding the sledgehammer out to her.

Sass immediately nods her head, more excited than I imagined she would be to do this. I watch as she pulls back and slams the hammer down. It does nothing but bounce back at her. I try to withhold my laugh.

"Put some muscle behind it," I tell her from where I stand over to the side, with an amused smile on my face.

"I *did*!"

I walk over and stand behind her, slipping my arms around her and putting my hands over hers where they meet the wood of the handle. We pull back together and let it fly. She shrieks as pieces of marble fly at her.

"There ya go," I encourage her.

"That's scary." She laughs as she wipes pieces of the stone from her clothing. "But it's fun. Let's do it again!"

I'm more than happy to help her, and I realize by doing this together, it's breaking down a barrier in our relationship. It's one I hope never stands in our way again—I hope we won't let it. Now that it's been toppled, it's our responsibility to make sure it never gets rebuilt.

CHAPTER TWENTY-ONE

Sass

I GRIN AS I look at my phone. The text Reed just sent me is making my cheeks flush and my thighs wet. This is a new facet to our relationship, but I can't say I don't like it.

I woke up this morning hard, remembering how you squeezed my cock so tight.

Between my thighs I can remember the feeling of how hard he was and how he shoved his body into mine. Thoughts like this shouldn't be running through my head at work, but I'm here by myself and I've got most of my work done. Justin isn't due back for at least an hour, so I can take this time to bask in the relationship Reed and I seem to be building with one another. I've never had a guy text me like this, flirt with me like this, and the fact it's Reed? It makes my heart pound. I never knew he was the type of guy to leave a woman in a puddle of goo, but here I am—in my own puddle. Thanks to him.

I can feel it. I text him back. *I'm still sore from the other night. A little bruised even, but I'm willing to take one for the team.*

That's not a lie either. I'm quickly coming to realize the people I've slept with before were boys. They were more worried about their pleasure and less worried about mine, not making sure I was satisfied. It wasn't equal opportunity. Reed? He's very much equal opportunity. Now I've had a man, I'm not sure I can ever go back. Let's face it; I never want to give Reed up.

We continue flirting by text, and we're at a particular hot group of texts when oddly he texts me with a *brb*. It feels abrupt, and I wonder what in the hell is going on.

Breathing out a frustrated sigh, I adjust in my seat and wonder if I can handle this. I'm playing with fire, and I could easily get burned if I'm not careful. I still don't know exactly what Reed's intentions are for me, and I'm still unsure of mine for him ultimately. We're playing this game with each other, but neither of us is sure of what the outcome will be. It seems dangerous, as if we shouldn't be doing this, but I don't want to give this up. For once in my life, I want this for me. I want something grown up and something that matters to the both of us. This matters more than anything in the world to me. I can't throw it away and tomorrow be good with my life. Even to myself, I can see I'm not a little girl anymore. It's time everybody take me seriously, because I'm taking myself seriously.

Reed

"WHAT THE FUCK are you doing here?"

I realize my voice is hard; it's harsh, not friendly at all, because there is no friendliness towards the woman standing in front of me. She should have showed up months ago—then I'd welcome her with open arms. I'd probably grovel like a pussy, begging her to take me back. Not today though, not today.

"Reed, come on, we have a history," Lacey says, a sickeningly sweet smile on her face.

There's something about the way she smiles at me that feels calculated; I can tell she knows exactly what she's doing. It makes my skin crawl, because I'm just now getting over the broken heart she left me with and moving on with my life. I want zero to do with this bitch. Our past is a fucked up mess of mistakes that should have been called off years before it was. I don't want her or the situation for anything in the world. I'm at the point, and I thank God I've come through on the other side.

"Forgive me if I'm not super excited about reliving history. You liked to have killed me when I kicked you out of our house. The past we share isn't exactly completely happy."

I stand up from my seat, towering over her as she looks up at me with calculating eyes. Before, I may have mistaken the look as helpless, one that said she needed a man to do things for her. One that would call on my need to be a man and help out a damsel in distress. Not anymore. I'm not stupid. Now I know who she is, I know what she is. She's calculating and she's sizing me up. I want this over with, and I want it done quickly.

"Again, I ask you what do you want."

Her smile fades, and I think she realizes I'm not as easy to manipulate as I once was. It gives me a feather for my cap and makes me push my chest out further as I cross my arms over it. She needs to see I'm no longer weak when it comes to her. I've finally got a brain of my own and a head on my shoulders. One that's not pussy-whipped where she's concerned.

"The house Taylor and I moved into needs some work, and we were wondering if you could do it for us. We know you're good at what you do and would give us a fair price." She says it with a straight face, and I have to blink twice to make sure I heard what she actually said to me.

I do everything I can to keep from laughing. Bitch is crazy. Which I kind of already knew, but this shit takes the cake.

"You can't afford me for what needs to be done to that house. You're better off going to someone who's starting out, and someone you don't have a fucking history with. Can you really trust I won't screw you over?" Because that would be what I would do. I would screw them over so hard, they wouldn't be able to even occupy the house—then I'd feel like a bastard, and I'd have to fix the problems I created. I can't let myself do this. The house Taylor put her into is a piece of shit, and this is evidence more than anything else that maybe she does like the drugs he said she does. She would have to be high to be okay living there. I know her standards, I know what she demanded of me, and if she's happy with what he's given her, shit has changed drastically.

She comes to stand next to me and puts her hand on my shoulder, leans in, and speaks to me in what I know she thinks is a sexy voice. "I can pay you in other ways, Reed. It was always good between us."

I smack her hand away and physically move her so she's not draped over me again. I smirk, hating myself for telling her this, but knowing it's the absolute truth. I won't lead her on, and I won't lie about what I have with Sass. She's turned me on in ways Lacey never had a snowball's chance in hell of doing, and I won't cheapen what she and I have together. I have to make Lacey see I don't even *entertain the fucking thought.* "Now I've had better, and know exactly what I was missing with you. Sorry, Lacey. It's over. I don't want a damn thing to do with you ever again."

Tears come to her eyes, and she truly looks heartbroken. These don't look like the tears she manufactures for people who don't let her have her way. I have to seriously wonder how many people in her life haven't given into her pouty face and whiney voice. It must hurt if she never hears it. I know she's never heard it from me before. Without another word, she turns and runs from my office.

Picking up my phone, I text Sass back. I need to see her, I need to be grounded in reality, and if there's anyone that can ground me, it's her.

Wanna go to Hank's tonight?

When she texts back *sure*, I know I'm right where I'm supposed to be at this time in my life. With a relief I didn't know I had, I realize the breakup with Lacey was a gift from God I'm not throwing back anytime soon.

CHAPTER TWENTY-TWO

Sass

I SWIPE THE Lolita red lip stain over my lips and smile at myself in the mirror. It's not often I decide to get dolled up. It's even less often I decide to wear what Morgan calls my blowjob-red lipstick, but tonight, I have a plan. In fact, I'm on a mission.

Looking at myself in the mirror, I know I'm hot. I don't pull out all the stops all the time, but I've done it tonight. Tonight I need something all mine; like I want to stake some sort of claim, and I'll be damned if Reed tells me no.

Grabbing up my curling wand, I work on curling the long pieces of hair that frame my face. My dark hair is getting a little lighter with the amount of time I've spent out in the sun this summer, and I like it. The natural highlights haven't been paid for this year, they've been earned. I've been careful to use sunscreen too, so the golden quality to my skin—that's another thing I've earned by hard work. It all feels good. Glancing down at my nails, I grin. I took the afternoon off to go get them done. They are Tiffany blue on all but my ring finger, which flashes a shimmering gold as I grab hold of my brush.

There's only one hairstyle I do well, and it's this one. I purposely make my curls all kinds of messy because I'm hoping Reed will mess them up when I'm on my knees and he's digging his hands into my hair.

Tonight he won't say no to me. I know he won't.

SITTING IN THE passenger seat of Reed's truck, I can't help but smile. I've wondered a lot since I became aware of my crush on him what it would be like to sit here. What it would be like to command his attention. Since we started "dating", I've always met him at his house, or he's met me somewhere. We haven't gone many places together, and when he said he'd pick me up, I jumped at the chance.

"You okay to eat at Hank's?" he asks as we drive on the main strip towards the bar.

The windows are down, and my hair is blowing in the warm, summer air, but I'm okay with that too. It's everything I ever wanted and ever thought it would be. I love that people can see me riding shotgun. I revel in it, because funny as it sounds, it's one of my dreams come true.

"Sounds good," I answer back over the sound of the wind coming through the open window. This is everything I've ever wanted in my life being handed to me on a silver platter. I wonder if maybe I shouldn't get so excited, maybe I should assume things will go downhill, but I can't. Not when I'm so high on the life I'm living right now.

His gaze is heated as his tongue brushes against his bottom lip. "If I haven't mentioned it, you look amazing tonight."

Looking down at myself, I try to see what he sees, but it's hard, to the point where I can't. I've always been the little girl chasing him, but now I'm the woman who's had him. I do something I've never done before. I point-blank ask him. "What do you see when you look at me?"

He adjusts in his seat, and I'm unsure if it's because I've put him on the spot or because I've affected him so strongly. I hope it's because I've affected him so strongly. It gives me a boost of self-esteem.

"An amazingly beautiful woman wearing a tight-ass tank top, perfect fucking ripped jeans, and fuck-me boots, with hair that makes me want to bury my face in it and take a deep breath. Do you have perfume there, or is it the natural scent you have? Every time I'm around you, I smell coconuts."

"It's my shampoo," I mumble, not sure at all how to handle what he's just told me. I've always been the same old Sass, and for him to see me as something different is empowering, but also a little scary. I push my thighs together and turn to face him, pulling my seatbelt away from my chest.

"You really see that when you look at me?"

We're at a stoplight, and Reed takes his eyes off the road long enough to rake his gaze over my body. His big hand comes off the wheel and he reaches over, caressing my cheek in the palm of his hand. The callouses and rough skin rub harshly against my softness, but it's soothing. If anything screams Reed, it's those strong, working man's hands.

"You're a gorgeous woman; I can't believe it took me this long to realize it."

There goes my heart. It's not playing in this game we've started. It's beating fast and strong and for him. If this ends, I'm dead, but I'm going to enjoy it while I can. I realize for the first time maybe the way I see myself and the way he sees me are two totally different things.

Behind us, a horn blares, and the moment is broken, but not before he leans forward to brush a kiss against my forehead.

"REED!" I SHRIEK as he swings me around the dance floor. He

pulls me closer, and I hook my arms around his neck, giggling as he hugs me close. My heart flutters against my chest, and looking at him, I can see how much fun he's having. It makes me happy, makes me hopeful.

"What?" He grins at me, the dimple in his left cheek showing. "You wanted to dance, Cassandra," he teases.

He's right, I *did* want to dance, but this feels so different than any other time we've hung out. We're here in front of half the town, and I've seen Lacey and Taylor here too. Justin sits over in the corner with a few guys from our crew and Morgan. This is public, this is for real, and it scares me because I feel this so acutely. Looking into Reed's eyes, I wonder if he feels the same way I do, but I'm scared to ask. There is a glimmer of something there that part of me knows is honest and true, but I don't want him to actually voice it. I'm afraid it won't be what I want, and then I'll be done for.

"You wanna stop?" he asks, his chest heaving against mine, his eyes sparkling in the dim lights of the bar.

"No." I shake my head. I never want to, but I keep those words to myself, shrieking again as he twirls me around the dance floor.

In this moment, the little girl who adored Reed becomes the woman who's fallen in love with Reed, and nothing has ever frightened me more.

CHAPTER TWENTY-THREE

Reed

S ASS HAS HAD a little too much to drink, and she giggles as she stumbles her way out of Hank's. I grab hold of her belt loop and pull her closer to me, making sure she has her footing.

"You okay?" I ask, taking a moment to look at her face. Her cheeks are flushed, her eyes are bright, and she's never looked more beautiful or alive to me than she does right here, right now.

She giggles again and pulls my face down to hers. "I'm perfect," she says one second before her mouth meets mine in a kiss. Her lips coax mine open, and her tongue invades the space between them. It's hot, how she's taking control, and I've sprung a chubby just thinking about what I can do to this woman, my woman, when I get her home. She hooks her fingers into the belt loops of my jeans, and before I realize what she's doing, she's pulled me to the side of Hank's. The only truck parked over here is mine. We've stayed a lot later than I meant to, and tomorrow is going to be a hell of a day at work for both of us.

I turn her towards the passenger side of the truck, popping the door open as I pull my lips away from hers. "C'mon, Sass, we'll move this to someplace a lot more private," I mumble, trying to tell both her and my dick to calm down.

"No." She spins me around and pushes me into the seat so

that I've got my feet on the running board. "Let me show you how much I want you, Reed." In that moment she sobers up, and I know immediately I'm done for. She has a plan, and the plan is me.

My eyes follow as she runs her hands up and down my thighs before focusing her attention on the space where my cock is attempting to make a tent in my jeans. She glances around and then looks back at me. The heat of the bar has smudged her mascara and eyeliner, but the red lip stain is still on there. Since I picked her up, I've wondered what her mouth would look like wrapped around my cock, but thinking about it brings back all the bad memories. I want to stop her as her fingers go to the button on my jeans and pop it open. The loosening against my junk lets me know my zipper is being lowered.

Her eyes meet mine. "Let me give you a good memory, baby," she coos. "Let me show you how this should be done. I want to know every time I wear this lipstick you think about this night here in Hank's parking lot." She tugs down my boxer briefs and jeans. "Remember what good head I gave to you. Replace the bad with the good."

Fuck it, why am I fighting against this? I use the back of the seat and the running board to help me lift my hips up so I can allow her to pull my clothes down to my knees. "If I get partially naked, then you do too, sweetheart."

Reaching down, I pull her tank top over her head; leaving her in the one of the hottest bras I've ever seen her wear. It's cut so low I can almost see her areola just from the movement of her chest. Her hand fists my cock, and she flashes a look up at me, a smirk showing on those red-lined lips before she bends over at the waist and envelopes me in her warm mouth.

"Fuck." I bite out harshly against gritted teeth, immediately shoving my fingers into her hair, pulling her down tighter against me. I forgot how fucking good this felt.

Sass

WRAPPING MY LIPS around his length feels like I've won a battle. It's something I have he never wanted to give, and to know he finally feels comfortable enough to do that makes me feel like the winner of the lottery. Using my hand, I run it up and down the part I can't fit in my mouth as I allow my throat to relax and take him deeper into the back.

His fingers are digging into my scalp, holding me down as he thrusts his hips up towards me, and I love it, because that means he's into it. Whatever preconceived notion he's had about it, whatever hang up prevented him from letting me do it before seems to be gone. I moan as I slip further down, using my tongue to run across the head, holding him in my mouth as I suck harder.

"Sass, that feels so good."

His hands work against my bra; he's pulling the cups down and exposing my tits to the night air. He pulls them forward, using them to envelope his cock as he pulls my mouth off of him.

"Just a second." He breathes deeply, panting. "Let me do this for just a second."

And he glides his wet length between my breasts, pushing up into them, fucking them hard. The look of concentration on his face is hot, especially when he pulls his bottom lip between his teeth. Eventually he opens his eyes and takes it all in.

"This is the hottest fuckin' thing I've ever seen, Sass. I can't believe you're lettin' me titty-fuck you in the parking lot of Hank's bar."

Neither can I, but this is the length I will go to in order to make this man happy. In order to let him know I trust him with every part of my being. He looks as if he's fighting something and then stops. "Your mouth again, please." He gulps a huge breath of air, and it takes a lot for him to ask this of me. I see he's grappling with the thoughts. It's probably a mental block he never thought he'd be able to get over. I'm proud of him; he's done it.

I offer him another smirk as I lean up to kiss him on the lips. I pull back, and before I go down again, I give him words that I've been wanting to give for a long time. "This is completely my pleasure, babe, and this time...don't stop until you come. I'll take it." The promise is there in my voice, and the way his eyes heat up, I know I've said the right thing.

This isn't about me, has never been about me, and it feels amazing to know I can be this selfless with him. That he'll take it and realize it's because I want to do it, not because I have to. This time when I go down, my mouth and throat are already relaxed, and I don't have to work his cock in the way I had to before. I immediately take him, bottoming out on the first push downward.

"Son of a bitch." He growls above me.

I don't think he was expecting that, so I pull back and do it again. My goal tonight is to completely rock his world. Using my free hand, I reach down and cup his balls in between my fingers. They tighten as I slowly pull them away from his body. Glancing up, I notice he's leaning back in the seat, almost lying completely down as he shoves his hips towards me. He's still got one hand tangled in my hair, holding me down over top of him, and the other is gripping the back of the seat. His abs expand and contract, mesmerizing me, as his stomach works overtime getting breath inside his lungs.

"Sass, fuck, I'm almost there," he warns me, his hips pumping faster.

Knowing he's closer, I double my efforts, running my tongue up and down his length, using my saliva to give me more lubrication, and digging my nails into his thighs. I urge him as I pull my mouth up, almost off, and then slide back down, hard.

"Fuck, fuck, fuck," he's chanting, as his balls draw up tight to his body, and I want him to come more than I've ever wanted anything in my life. Sucking extra hard, I hollow out my cheeks, he moans, and his heat spills down my throat.

His fingers grip in my hair, pulling tightly, holding me there as I take everything he's got to give. As I swallow, I feel like I've run a marathon. Finally lifting my mouth off of him, I rest it on his stomach, hearing his labored breathing, and give myself a pat on the back.

Something tells me this may have been the most important blowjob of my life.

CHAPTER TWENTY-FOUR

Sass

THIS DAY HAS been forever long; I'm tired and a little hung over. Instead of being at work, I want to be with Reed. He let me break down the final wall he'd been holding onto when he let me give him the blowjob last night. I've wanted nothing more all day than to leave work and go to his house to be with him. That thought is what's getting me through the day.

The late night out dancing at Hank's with Reed has me feeling it this afternoon. My legs and thighs are sore and so are my arms. The arms, though? I think they're soreness is from where Reed let me pleasure him, where I held myself up over him for so long. I pull up to the job Justin's texted me, and immediately realize I'm at the auto shop Taylor owns. This has really bad idea written all over it. I wonder if Justin took this appointment or if it's one our answering service took while both he and I were on a job. I would hope if Justin had taken that call, or known exactly who this was, he would have told Taylor to shove this up his ass. No money is worth this.

I contemplate getting back in the truck, but he sees me and yells at me. "Sass, I've been waiting on you."

Fucking great. "Hey." I wave. "What can I help you with?" I'm doing my best to be professional; because if I have to be here, I need to treat him with the same respect I would treat anyone else, because no matter what, this is our job. If he starts spreading bad juju around, then it will affect our bottom line, and that's not something we can ever afford. Each penny, each dollar is needed at Straight Edge because we are a seasonal business, and I can't let the personal affect the professional. It's hard though to not look at him and want to both smack him for ruining a relationship and also want to hug him because he gave me a chance at the relationship I've always wanted. It's a hell of a place to be in.

He waits for me to catch up with him before he answers. Putting his hands on his hips, he offers me a smile. It makes my skin crawl. Out of Reed and Taylor, Taylor has never made me feel one-hundred-percent comfortable. Ever since the summer I turned thirteen.

My brother's best friends are over, and all I want to do is layout in the backyard, but they've already taken over the space. Every Saturday they come over and run football plays. It's so annoying. I've complained to my mom about it, but she's busy making sure my dad is taken care of, and she can't be bothered with this. If my dad weren't sick, I know he would run them off.

Squaring my shoulders, I grab my iPod, a towel, and the suntan oil and make my way to the backyard. I do my best to ignore them. With my earbuds in and sunglasses over my eyes, it's not hard. For two hours I lie under the sun's warmth, turning every thirty minutes, without any of them bothering me. That's when my silence is broken; a sharp tap on my behind startles me. I lift my head up, taking the earbuds out, and turn around, glaring at whoever this is. I huff out a breath and roll my eyes when I notice Taylor blocking the sun. I cross my arms to let him know the interruption wasn't appreciated.

"Stop that." I look around for my brother or Reed, but they are no-where to be found.

"You're really growin' up, Sass." He's smiling down from where he

stands over me.

The way he smiles makes my skin crawl, and I know I have to hit him with what others have commented is my sassy mouth. "Too bad you're the absolute last person I want to notice I'm growin' up."

I grab my towel with all my stuff and run into the house. Never again will I be alone with Taylor. I'll make sure of it.

Until today, I've never been alone with him again. He's talking, and I'm doing my best to let the memories go and act like I'm really listening.

"Obviously I do my own lawn care. It's not like Justin would touch this place with a ten-foot pole after what I did to his best friend in the whole wide world. I'm not stupid enough to think y'all will take over the lawn maintenance. While I kind of accept that, even though I think it's shitty business on your part, I do need to know how much it would be to lay some sod. I looked in the tri-county area, and y'all are the only ones who do that, so either you do it, or you blackball me. Whatever, but I need to make what once was my junkyard valuable. I've removed all the piece-of-shit cars, and now I need for it to look good. There's a loan I need to take out on this place, and it's got to score well in aesthetic. Believe me, I need your help; otherwise, I wouldn't have called."

I follow him at a distance. Something about this doesn't sit well with me. I can't tell if he's bullshitting me or not; he gives me the heebie jeebies since that day in the backyard of my parents' house. I want this done, and I want back in the truck and safe at the office.

I'm looking down at my iPad, making notes. When I look up, I don't see him in front of me any longer. "Fuck," I hiss as I chase after where I think he went. This is really not what I want to be doing this morning. *Keep your head in the game. The quicker you get this done, the quicker you can go back to the office.* Which is where I want to be now. Forget being with Reed. Right now, I want to be out of here and on my way back to the office.

As I go around the corner of the building, I still can't see him, but suddenly I'm pressed against the wood, a hand at my throat. Gasping for air, I'm fighting against the hold, wondering what in the fuck is going on and why I've been slammed like a ragdoll against a hard surface. It's unforgiving, and I do my best to try and minimize impact, but he loosens his hold and then tightens again. This is the fear that scared me when I was in the backyard with him as teenager; this is the dread that turned my stomach when I pulled up to this building today.

Taylor is up in my face, whispering against my ear. "Lacey went to see Reed the other day, and I need you to pass a message along to him. You let him know she's mine. If he fucks with what's mine, I'll fuck with what's his. I got her; I can get you even easier," he threatens, squeezing so tightly my feet come up off the ground.

My legs dangle, and I'm more scared than I've ever been in my life. I try to think of a way out of this, but he's caught me off guard, and there's no way for me to break free that I can see. Desperately, I thrash my head back and forth, trying to break his hold against me. When I finally do, he drops me to the ground. Grateful, I suck in deep breaths of air, trying to fill my lungs.

"What the fuck is wrong with you?" I gasp, putting my hand to my throat, rubbing where it aches and trying to figure out if this guy has lost his ever-loving mind. I grab my phone and wonder if I should call 9-1-1, but at this point, I'm too confused about what's happening.

"You let Reed know I got Lacey, I can get you too. I know Lacey went to see him the other day. Just let him know I'm keeping tabs. By the way, you looked real good last night givin' Reed head in his truck. I've been thinkin' all day about what it would be like if you gave it to me. Just know the option is there, in case you ever want to indulge," Taylor says, like he's proud of himself.

I want to tell him his confession borders on being a stalker, but I'm scared I might end up back against the wall, and I'm worried if I go back there, this time I may not come out of this. I'm sick at the fact he saw me doing that to Reed last night. Yeah, I knew we were out in the open, I knew it was a risk we were taking, but I never in a million years thought Taylor would see it. The fact he wants me to do it to him makes me want to throw up.

At the same time, my head is spinning. Lacey went to see Reed? He never shared that information with me, and it fucking pisses me off. I'm being punished for something I know absolute nothing about and I should. Last night, it felt like Reed and I turned a corner, we went from being pretend to real. The way he looked at me, the way he trusted me to go down on him, the way my heart pounded when he looked at me; it was different. It felt real, and now I'm questioning all of it. I'm wondering if I've been played. This fucking hurts, but I have to get out of here, I have to get away from Taylor, and I have to figure out what's going on. I have to make some sort of plan, and I need to talk to Reed.

"Kiss my ass." I get up off the ground and do the one thing I know I can. I kick him in the balls, yelling as I do it. "You ever put your hands on me again, and not only will Reed and Justin beat the shit out of you, I'll shove your balls so far up your ass you'll be coughing them out of your esophagus." I gasp, still trying to catch my breath.

I'm livid as I stomp back to my truck. My hands shake as I crank the ignition, and once again I'm pissed I've been reduced to this. I'm not the kind of woman who lets a man put hands on her. I've never been weak before, but this came at me from out of nowhere. I wasn't prepared, and now I feel like I've been used as a sacrificial lamb because I wasn't warned. Tears escape my eyes as I throw gravel and squeal tires out of the parking lot. There is only one thought running through my head. Reed has some explaining to do.

CHAPTER TWENTY-FIVE

Reed

I AM SO freakin' ready to see Sass. Before last night, at Hank's, I didn't need to have to see her every day, but everything changed last night. She broke down a barrier I wasn't fully aware existed, but I know today it's gone. I'm lighter and more at peace with my life. This is a feeling I haven't had in such a long time.

Today I haven't seen her, and I haven't been able to text her. I fucking miss her. Saying I miss her is an understatement. I don't know where this came from; it came on so gradually I didn't notice, and now it's hitting me full-force in the chest. She's become a part of my life, something I didn't anticipate— something I count on and look forward to. I look forward to seeing her, I look forward to talking to her, I look forward to her texts. I like her spending a few nights here and there in my bed, I love hearing her laugh, and I enjoy fishing with her. She lets me be myself, and even more, she makes me better than I've ever been before.

There's a part of me that wonders if this will last or if it's because our relationship is new. This whole situation started in a way that wasn't real, but the feelings are turning very real. It's one of the scariest situations I've ever been in, because I'm not in control of this. It's hard for me to put myself out there again to another woman, but I know I have to. I don't know if I want to be completely honest with myself or not. Being honest with myself isn't something I've been in a long time because I was so wrong about Lacey. I've not felt like I've been able to trust myself since it happened, and I'm gun shy. Right now I'm the person I trust the least, and that's a difficult place to be in, one I never imagined I would be in. My heart and mind both know it's time to start being real and stop being polite. I need to give Sass this benefit of the doubt, though. If there's anyone who deserves it, it's her. For once I'll push my fears aside and I'll give her what she needs, what I need, and I hope like hell she's on board with it.

The sound of a car coming up the drive has me looking over my living room like a mad man. I hope I cleaned up enough, even though I'm not sure why I care. This is Sass...this is just Sass. I know it's crazy to worry about that tonight after all we've been through together in the past few weeks. But tonight I want to make a good impression on her. She's bringing pizza, I have the beer, and hopefully we'll be having a chill night at home. I try to calm my breathing and my heart, but I've come to this amazing conclusion and had such an epiphany that this woman means a lot to me. I want to shout it from the rooftops, but I don't know if she feels the same. *Play it cool, Reed.*

"Hey," I greet her as I walk out onto my porch.

Lately, I've noticed she takes my breath away. It's been something gradual, and another thing I hadn't been expecting. Before, I was pushing it aside, but tonight, I let the feeling wash over me, I let myself experience it. Her hair is down around her face, she isn't wearing a lick of makeup, and her jeans and T-shirt are both well worn. They fit her like a second skin.

"Hey." She gifts me with a shaky smile as she ascends the steps, holding a pizza box.

I lean in to take it from her, sneaking in a kiss on her cheek.

She melts into me for a moment, sighing softly. "You okay?" I ask, because that's not like her. She's always enjoyed when I pay her attention, but the way she melted into me was like I was her lifeline. Not that I don't want to be that for her. It's unusual and sets off warning bells in my head.

Her voice is thin and wobbly as she pushes out the words. "Just a hard day at work."

"Wanna talk about it?" After all, that's what I'm here for. I want to be everything she needs, whether it be the shoulder to cry on, the arms to hold her tight, or the good lay in bed she wants. Whatever it is, I'm her man.

We make our way into the house, heading straight for the kitchen, and I wonder if she'll notice. I've been hard at work today too.

"Oh, Reed, you changed the countertop. I *love* this stone one!"

The praise feels good, and I love she loves it, but I know a change of subject when I hear one. "Great," I set the pizza down and grab some paper plates. "Now, you wanna tell me what happened at work?" I don't like the fact she's hiding something from me. I want her to be able to talk to me about anything and everything. Whatever happened to her, I want to make this better.

She puts a piece of pizza on her plate and grabs a beer out of the fridge. She's become more at home in my home, and I like that. It makes me feel good. That I've made a place where she can be comfortable too. She takes a fortifying drink of the beer and picks a pepperoni off the pizza.

"I had a meeting with Taylor today."

The way she says it makes my hair stand on end, and immediately my blood boils. I don't even like to hear his name spoken. I know that's not fair to her, but I don't trust him. I never will again, and I don't think it's fair for her to bear the brunt of my annoyance, but she's going to have to. "Really?" Suddenly my appetite is nonexistent, and I throw my piece of pizza onto the paper plate.

"Don't be like that." She blows a breath out her nose. "It's not like I wanted to do it, but he's a paying customer. Things got weird." She shakes as she puts her arms around her middle, her drink and food forgotten.

"In what way, Cassandra?" My voice is harder than I want it to be, but damn if this doesn't piss me the fuck off.

I can see her wrestling with this. I can see her debating if she wants to go with the truth or not. That fucking pisses me off too. "Don't you dare even think about lying to me. I trust you. I trust you more than I ever trusted Lacey, and if you break that trust, you'll never get it back." It's all or nothing with me, and I can't change how I am.

Her face goes white. "You can't make demands, and you can't out of the blue tell me you trust me more than Lacey. That's not fair," she argues.

"You wanna know what's not fair? Him already stealing one love of my life isn't fair."

I can't get enough breath in my lungs. This hurts, knowing she's not being honest with me. It hurts more than I ever thought it would. "What the fuck happened, Sass?"

"He cornered me." She turns so she's not facing me. "Told me he could have me as easily as he had Lacey. He shoved me up against the wall and held me there so I couldn't breathe."

I walk over to her, grasp her at the bicep, and turn her around so she faces me. I'm angrier than I've been in a long time, but I can't get over the fact he's threatened to steal her from me. "That's not gonna happen. You got that?"

There are tears in her eyes, and it pulls at my heart, but I need to know. What's it going to be? Will she leave me just like Lacey did? Out of every conversation we've had, this one right here is the most significant in my mind.

She shakes her head in a "no" fashion. "I don't want it to happen, Reed," she yells, her voice pleading. I hate I've reduced her to this, but dammit, I need to know. "All I want is you, all I've ever wanted is you."

I'm all over her. I need to know how much she wants me, I need to know he's not going to take away another integral piece of my life. I won't survive it. Lacey I survived, I carved out an existence, and I forced myself to live. Sass—she's become too much of a part of my life. If she left me, if Taylor got to her, I wouldn't be able to take it. I try to show her in the way my lips dominate hers, and I hope like hell she can understand what I'm trying to convey.

CHAPTER TWENTY-SIX

Sass

NEVER IN MY life have I been aroused by or with a man this aroused before, but I get the feeling this isn't about pleasure. It's about staking a claim. Reed is coming at me like a dog in heat, and I'm not sure I can handle him. Something about the way I let him know what happened with Taylor has got him all over me. I can't help but be okay with that. This is what I've wanted all along—him to care about me so much he would do anything it takes to have me.

I press my head back against the pillow on his mattress and expose my throat to him, encouraging him to take what he wants, what he needs. I'm not even sure how we got here, to the bedroom. The last thing I remember is being in the kitchen. I don't know when he picked me up and brought me up here, but I'm totally on board with whatever he wants to do. He's consuming me as he runs his whiskered face against my jawbone. I moan as he nips the skin, using his hand to tilt my head back.

"What is this?" he asks, his eyes dark as he sees the bruises on my neck. His tone is no-nonsense, but it doesn't scare me the way Taylor's did.

"Taylor lifted me up against the barn wall." I'm holding on to his shoulders tightly. I don't want Reed to leave me; I don't want this to send him over the edge. "I told him if he tried to do anything like that again, I'd shove his balls so far up his ass he'd be spitting them."

He chuckles against my skin before grasping my wrists and bringing my hands over my head, entwining our fingers, putting our palms together. "That's my girl, but I think I'll be having a few words with the fucker myself."

Hearing him call me his girl does weird things to me. It makes me want to believe things that probably are never going to come true. It makes me want to write our names together on a notebook and see what they would look like if we were married. This is the type of stuff I can't handle anymore; this is the type of stuff I need to get a grip on.

"Reed, love me," I beg him. I don't even realize the words that have come out of my mouth and I don't think he has either. I need him to ground me.

"I should withhold myself to let you understand my anger about him pushing you up against a barn and you not telling me," he grits out between his teeth.

Suddenly I realize he's angry. He's pissed at me because I haven't been honest, because I didn't run to him with this problem I had. I can see him wrestling with himself, and it's then I give in. I let my arms go slack, let my hands go slack against his, and I give myself over. Because in some strange way I want him to take control, and I want to see what he'll do with it. "Whatever you think I deserve." And I mean it, because I'm an idiot for going out there and being alone with Taylor when I knew he made me feel uncomfortable. I feel like an even bigger idiot for letting my feelings get in the way of whatever this is with Reed, and I need a reality check.

He pulls me up off the bed, putting me on my knees in front of him. Running his hands down my side, he catches my shirt and yanks it over my head. I look at him, trusting him to do with me what he wants, and I think it's the hunger in my eyes that convinces him. A growl escapes his throat as he palms my breasts, pushing them up above the cups of my bra. The tips rub against the edges of the lace, frustrating me.

Leaning down, his tongue comes out from between his lips to soothe the ache that's set up shop at the ends of my nipples. They are their own nerves, and I need him to soothe the burn. I thrust myself into his mouth, dig my hands in his hair, and hold him in place. The large palm that was gripping my tit is now moving down my back to my ass. I want his skin on mine, so I reach down and undo the button on my jeans before reaching over and undoing the button on his.

I whimper when he puts his hands down the loosened back of mine, pulling the waistband of my panties tight against his hand. It puts pressure on my core, and I'm so turned on it makes me groan, and I rake my fingernails down his back in response. I fight as I try to take his shirt off, but he doesn't want to release my nipple. He has a tight hold on my flesh, and I know tomorrow I'll wear the bruises and the love nips of this encounter around like badges of honor.

I'm grinding my body down against the fabric he's pulling tightly against my pussy, and I think I can come from the pressure alone. When I am almost there, he stops gripping the fabric, releases my flesh, and his mouth leaves my body. I fall back against the covers, because his big hands were holding me up, and now he's left me.

"Reed." I gasp, my nipples tight against my skin, my core throbbing against the arousal there. Surely to God he won't leave me hanging.

He stands up and gets rid of his clothes before he reaches over and grabs me by the ankles, pulling my jeans off. It's disconcerting the way he doesn't speak as he grabs my panties and pulls them off as well. I make a move to take the bra off, but he puts his hands overtop mine.

"Leave that on."

His voice is dark, and I'm trying to decide if he's exorcising some demons or if this is just the way he is sometimes. I don't have enough experience with him to know yet. I stop what I'm doing when he pulls me to him, and without any kind of fanfare, sticks his hand between my legs. I moan when two fingers insert themselves inside me.

"Ohhh, Sass. We're gonna have some fun." He takes those same two fingers out, putting them to his lips and then enveloping them with his mouth. His tongue swirls, licking my essence off himself. It's probably the hottest thing I've ever seen in my life, causing my stomach to clench and my nipples to harden even further. This is the kind of bad boy I knew he could be but hadn't been privy to. These are the actions fantasies are made of.

My mouth hangs open as I watch. Then I'm flipped over and I'm facing the headboard. His big body comes up behind me, and like that, I feel him inside me. His hands grip the wood of the headboard as he rocks into me. He's large, and it hurts for a second until I will myself to relax. Right now he doesn't care; this is all about him and his need to know I'm his.

"Fucking Taylor," he forces through clenched teeth. The tone of his voice is irritated anger, and I let him rage, because I don't know what else to do. "Thinking he's going to take something that's mine again? Like hell. You're mine, and I'm not giving you up to anyone, much less him."

He's muttering, and I'm not sure if he even knows what he's saying, but he's owning me, and I'm not even ashamed about it. This is what I've wanted him to do for years, since I knew what sex was. He's going after what he wants, and that's a turn-on for me.

"I'm yours." I'm not sure if he can hear, since my head is turned, the pillow muffling my words.

The sound of the headboard hitting the wall is something I don't think I'll ever forget. I remember someone in one of my college classes telling me that's how you knew you were getting it good. I'm getting it better than good, though, I realize, because his knees have widened my legs. It's causing my clit to rub against the sheet underneath us every time he pushes in and pulls back. I want to turn my head and look at him, but I can't. My knees are slipping down the mattress, and he's got hold of the headboard in one hand, my bra strap in the other, and he's using both of those things for leverage to slam into me.

This should hurt, and I know it will tomorrow, but fuck if I don't want this right now.

"C'mon, Reed," I encourage him. I want to scream out I bet Lacey didn't let him fuck her like this—Lacey seems like she's too straight-laced, but I don't want to ruin the dream-like state we're in. I don't want this to end.

He's pushing faster and faster inside of me, his abs tightening against my back, and I know he's going to be hot and warm inside me at any minute, so I concentrate on tightening my own muscles, holding my breath, digging my fingers into the sheets so that I can move myself against them in my own rhythm.

He spills, and it's enough to send me off too, and as he breathes heavily against my back and I realize just how chafed my nipples are, I also realize I could never trust another man to use me this way and enjoy it.

Another thing Reed Shamrock has ruined for Cassandra Straight.

CHAPTER TWENTY-SEVEN

Reed

I 'M PISSED AND emotionally raw. Pissed because of the way I treated Sass last night. I should never have taken her that hard, especially after the day she had, but I couldn't help myself. I couldn't help the need I had to assert my power over her. It was one of the most intense experiences of my life, and while I feel guilty, I can't help but be thankful for it at the same time.

I'm emotionally raw because I faced some truths. Looking at those handprints on her skin, I know now what she means to me. I know the extremes I'll go to, in order to keep this woman safe and with me. Which is why I'm at Taylor's body shop at seven a.m. this morning. As soon as I pulled in, I saw his truck. I know he's here. I just have to find him. Walking around the side of the building, I wonder if this is where he approached Sass. Is this where he saw where she wasn't paying attention and went in for the kill? I'm already raging, and I know I don't have to think much about it to fucking detonate.

"Taylor!" I yell because I don't want to play this game of cat and mouse. I want him to come out from whatever rock he's crawled under, and I want to face him man to man. "Taylor!"

The side door opens, and he comes stumbling out, smoking what appears to be a hand-rolled joint. "What the *fuck* do you want?" he asks, looking up at me.

This is one time when I'm really thankful for my height advantage. Plowing towards him, I knock the joint out of his hand, slam the door, and push him up against it. "How's it goin'?" My tone is conversational, but I can tell by the wild look in his eyes he knows I'm not here to make small talk—any kind of talk really.

"That was expensive weed, you asshole, and it was my last little bit of it."

The fact he's worried this much about drugs tells me more than anything about how far he's fallen. I wonder if Lacey knows this. I wonder if she realizes what a piece of shit she's sharing a bed with, and I have to remind myself it's none of my business. It's an epiphany though, because I realize I'm worried as a friend, not as an ex-lover.

"I don't give a shit about that." I move my hand up against his windpipe and use the leverage to pick him up off the ground. "Does this seem familiar to you? *This* is what I give a shit about."

"Reed, I was playing around." His words are strained against my hand.

I tighten my grip. "Playing around? You don't play around and leave handprints on her throat. You're lucky she didn't call the fucking cops on you. You're lucky I didn't. What the fuck is wrong with you?" I loosen my grip and let his feet hit the ground because I want to hear him.

"That's something you would do, right? You're perfect, and you never want to get your hands dirty. All the stupid shit we did in high school and after, and golden boy Reed never once suffered the consequences."

I know what he's talking about. Taylor has been arrested more than once for public intoxication because he likes to drink a little too much. I've been with him numerous times, but never

135

gotten arrested myself because I've always been respectful and never been above the legal limit. That's the difference between us, I know my limits.

"Fuck you."

"You moved on really quick, didn't you? Sass has always been a hot piece of ass."

That's it, I've been nice, but those words piss me off. I pick him up higher than before with one hand and pull back with the other. When my fist hits his nose, it's the most satisfying crack I have ever heard. Even more satisfying than the one I gave him when I caught him with Lacey. Blood is pouring again, and I drop him down on the ground as I let go.

"Motherfucker, Reed. This is twice you've broke my damn nose." He's holding his nose again, bent at the waist.

"Ask me if I care." I step over him and walk back to my truck.

"You don't know what I saw, Reed. Maybe you should be more careful in parking lots, my man."

I rage, and I run back over to him, lifting him up by the collar of his shirt, cracking my knuckles against him one more time, and making sure I stomp on his stomach. He doubles over in pain and groans, saying he thinks he's going to throw up.

My work here is done.

Sass

JUSTIN LOOKS AT me as he enters the office, and I can tell he's surprised at what I look like. I'm a little surprised myself. I tried to cover it up, but I have whisker burn on my jawline and two hickeys. One on my neck and one on my earlobe; not to mention the love bites my clothes are concealing. I have bruises on my thighs, and I'm sore—thoroughly sore. I know I look like I've had the most amazing sex of my life, but last night was probably the most emotionally painful encounter I've ever had. It's taking everything I have to hold back the tears that are threatening and have been threatening since I woke up this morning and made a quick exit from Reed's house.

"Damn, Cassandra." He shakes his head as he gets a good look at me. I don't know if he's ashamed or if he wants to give me a high-five.

"I don't even want to talk about it." I'm raw today. Last night took a lot emotionally out of me, and I'm not sure how much I have left to give anyone else. I don't even know right now how much I have left to give myself.

"Tough shit, you're gonna hear it, and if he were here, he would be hearing it too. In fact, I may find his ass and give him an earful. You're my goddamn sister, he should know better than to treat you like this."

When Justin gets on his high horse, it's hard to knock him down, and I want nothing more than to do that right now. But it's just another thing I don't have in me at this moment, another thing I can't force myself to do. It's better this way.

"Where do you see this heading?" he asks, looming over me. "Do you really think Reed is gonna give anyone else a ring after what happened with Lacey? Do you think you're special, Sass? Do you think you're the one? I've seen this out of him since he started dating. He moves on, and he moves on with everything he has. But it doesn't stick."

"Shut up," I yell at him, my eyes watering. I know all of these things. I've had these talks with myself. I don't need him to throw this in my face too. This is one time in my life where I don't need him to be straight with me, I don't need him to be honest. I need him to be my big brother and tell me everything is going to be okay, the same way he did when our dad died.

"No, it's time you face this. How do you think this is going to end?" He looks down on me, and I can see his disappointment. It's devastating to me.

I swallow against the lump in my throat, looking up at my big brother. The one who's been there for me so many times since our dad died, the one who's protected me. I know he's doing the same here, but fuck, this hurts so much more than I thought it would. I'm not prepared for this; I'm not prepared for his disappointment in me, or mine in Reed. I'm completely lost, and I'm not sure I know how to find the old Sass. The one who would bite back with a smart-ass retort. She's not here at the moment; I'm not sure she'll ever be back. That forecast is looking cloudy.

"I want to end up spending the rest of my life with him, but I'm scared I'm going to end up alone and wishing things were different. Hoping like hell he realizes I'm not Lacey," I admit, hugging my arms to my body.

"At least you're honest with yourself, but I won't be there to pick either one of you up from this. You're blindly in love with him, and he's falling for you, but neither of you want to admit it to each other. This shit is stupid. You need to be honest with one another—if not, it's going to implode. I know how this goes." He throws his hands up and heads out of the office, obviously done with this conversation.

Unfortunately, I know how this ends too. My heart broken.

CHAPTER TWENTY-EIGHT

Reed

I PULL AT the collar of the shirt I'm wearing; cursing the fact I have a business meeting on such a hot fucking day. Two days after my encounter with Taylor and my anger still has yet to cool. Taylor has pissed me off, and I'm pissed off at myself because of how I treated Sass. It's a double-edged sword I haven't figured out how to navigate yet. I can't get his words out of my head—that he could get her as easily as he got Lacey. And I can't seem to forget the way Sass looked when I came inside her. I'm halfway ashamed at the way I made love to her. It wasn't soft, it wasn't tender. I took my anger out on her, and I'm feeling like a total bastard. I've felt like a total bastard since I woke up and again found her gone. I wonder if this is the kind of man I've turned into. When did this start? When did I lose the piece of myself that believed in love and flowers and caring more about your partner? It's time to take a hard look at my life, and that begins with me.

Right now, though, right now I need to focus on business and not the tattered shreds of my love life.

"Reed?"

I look up and see Mr. Stanton, the one who's coordinating the planned subdivision, the one with whom I have the meeting. Luckily for me, Alexa has taken the helm on hiring the new help, and at least that's been taken care of. It's time for me to get my game face on and deal with business.

"Sir." I hold out my hand. "It's good to see you."

"You too, Reed. I hope you have some good news and some good plans for us." He's looking at me like I hold the world in my hands, and I guess in a way I do. I'm going to tell him whether what he wants to do is feasible or not. I have the option of telling him yes or no. This is one part of my life I do have control over, one part I know I won't fuck up. I need this today, more than I've ever needed it before.

I hold up my hand where I carry a folder holding blueprints, mock-ups, and anything else about which the man can ask me. I'm prepared, like I always am when it comes to my business. I don't understand why I can't be this way in my personal life too. "I've been hard at work. I hope you like what we've done." When I say we, I mean Sass too, because there's one thing this woman is, and it's a partner in everything with me.

"What's got your attention so preoccupied?" Sass asks as she leans over the back of the couch.

The two of us are in my living room, relaxing after our long day at work. That day, however, is not done for me, and I hope she'll understand. I hope she doesn't fly off the handle the way Lacey used to.

"These plans for the subdivision. They wanted me to come up with some mock houses so they could see what they would be working with. I haven't had time to make it to the office in the past few weeks, and these are due soon. I wanted to get a head start on them, so I figured this was something I could do while we watched TV." I shrug. "I hope you don't mind."

"Not at all." She moves her legs off the couch so she's got her feet next to mine.

She has a seat on the floor next to me, folding her legs up Indian style, leaning her head against my shoulder. Her eyes run over the drawing, and they light up as she obviously gets an idea. "You should let me draw in some flowerbeds and let them see what landscaping will do for it. I think it'll give it more curb appeal and make it more eye-catching."

That's an idea I hadn't thought of, and I'm all for it. "Yes, please do that. It'll be easier for me to tell him the person who's drawn all of this is going to be available to do it."

I sit back and watch as she takes control of my plans and works her magic. This is a different situation for me, and I can't say I hate it. Having her here, working side by side with me has made this one of the best nights of my life.

I'm banking on it. The plans I've drawn up will allow both RS Construction and Straight Edge to grow. It's important to me this happens. There are families and life-long relationships depending on this.

"Let's go talk about it." He ushers me through the door, and I put my game face on. This is where I excel, and I refuse to let my friends down. I've done enough letting people down for the time being. This is where I need to man up and prove to myself I'm a winner.

THE MEETING WENT well, contracts were signed, and one is being sent over to Straight Edge right now. It's a good feeling to know I can possibly help my friends secure a contract that will help make their business grow. I hope it allows Justin to make changes so he can encourage the growth of the business and stabilize the cash flow. It's something we both always worry about. Our work, in this industry, is fickle, and it's a guessing game as to how things will be from year to year. Thinking about Justin makes me think about Sass. I wonder, not for the first time, what the hell is going on with her. I wonder what she's doing, if she's thinking of me, and if I'm still in the shit house with her. By all accounts, of what I can remember about myself,

I damn well should be. My cell phone rings beside me, interrupting my thoughts. I'm on auto-pilot at this point, and I grab it, answering without looking.

"RS Construction, this is Reed."

A crying voice greets me, and for a moment I'm paralyzed with fear, until I realize it isn't Sass. It's Lacey. My heart slows down, and I'm not in complete panic mode—now I wonder what in the hell she wants.

"Reed, I'm at your office. I need help." Her voice is thick with tears.

This is her damsel-in-distress voice. She uses it when she wants to get something. I've heard it all too much over the years. I roll my eyes and do my best not to yell at her just to scare her off. I want her gone, and I'm going to have to brace myself for whatever it is she's going to throw at me. "I'll be there in a second; I'm pulling onto the street right now."

As I pull into the parking lot, I realize I don't want to do this. I don't want to mess with her anymore. If someone had told me I would be at that point in my life, I would have laughed at them, but I've realized she's not what I want—maybe she's never been what I want. Maybe I went with it because it was what was expected of me and not because it was what my heart said.

Getting out of my truck, I walk towards her and cautiously ask her. "What's wrong?"

She's crying—huge crocodile tears. I've also seen these a few times in my life.

"I made a huge mistake." She runs up to me, throwing her arms around me, pressing herself into my body. "I should never have left you."

At one time I wanted to hear these words from her; I would have died or killed to hear these words from her. Now? They mean jack shit to me. They mean less than jack shit to me. I want out of this situation, and I want out of it yesterday. This has bad idea written all over it.

"What happened?" I ask, trying to keep the mocking tone out of my voice, but it's a struggle. "Did he not give you a piece of jewelry you want?"

Her face screws up as she tightens her arms around my neck. "You make it sound like I'm materialistic, that I don't have feelings. It's much more than that. He won't give me the wedding I want. That's the symbol of our love, and he doesn't want it to be what I want it to be. It hurts my feelings," she cries.

I laugh, trying to remove her arms from where they are locked around me. "We both know you'll run back to him. I was giving you the wedding of your dreams. I built you the house of your dreams, and I still couldn't keep you. This is a shit excuse because something's clicked with you and you realize you no longer have any kind of chance of us getting back together. Now you're scared. Trust me, you and your boyfriend, you're perfect for one another. You think you want me, but you don't. You never did, Lacey. We weren't good for each other." And for the first time, I realize, this is what Lacey does. She moves from one person to the next, depending on who she can latch onto at one time. She always has to feel wanted and needed, and whoever can give her that is her person.

"I do," she argues, and I'm too slow to miss her lips as they descend on mine.

I'm trying like hell to make her let go, but she's got hold of me. A car pulls up, and I have a horrible feeling in the pit of my stomach. "Stop," I plead against her lips.

"So this is how it's going to end, huh?"

My blood runs cold when Sass gasps out a really loud *motherfucker*, and I know this is it. She won't believe me, will never allow me to explain, will never give me a shot after this. Whatever we had is over, because she will leave and never look back.

"Have a nice life, Reed." She flips me off as she gets back in her car.

I turn to Lacey, wiping her lipstick off my lips. She's grinning, because she knows exactly what she's done. She's proud of herself, and I want to hit her. If she were a man, I would wipe the floor with her. "You're a stupid bitch. Get the fuck off my property."

"With pleasure."

I watch as she leaves, pissed I fell for her games again and scared to death I'm never going to get Sass to trust me after this. I hop in my truck and follow her to wherever it is she's going.

CHAPTER TWENTY-NINE

Reed

WE END UP at her apartment building. I pull in behind her, blocking her from leaving as she parks. I don't want her to be able to let me get out of my truck, and her back out of the parking space. "Let's go upstairs and talk about this." I'm trying to avoid the scene I know is coming. This is a scene I had hoped to avoid all the way around.

"No." She shakes her head. "We can do this here or not at all." She folds her arms over her chest and stands her ground. Her chin juts up at me, and I want to let her know how proud I am of her for standing tall, but the other part of me wants to tell her to stop being so fucking stubborn, that this is not what she thinks it is.

I don't understand why she wants to do this where other people can hear it. Then it hits me, she thinks this is the big break up. She wants the stage; she wants people to hear it and to know we're over. Sass still thinks I'm playing around with this, that it's a game. And why wouldn't she? I haven't been honest with her. I've internalized all my feelings; I haven't once spoken out loud what I've been realizing when it comes to her, and with a cold reality, I know she's not going to believe me now. She's going to think I'm saving face, and that's not at all what I'm doing. I'm trying to save my sanity.

"No, Sass, I don't want this," I try to let her know my feelings are true; this stopped being a game for me a long time ago. I can see in her eyes though she's not getting it. She's sticking to her part, and this is killing me. I don't know how to fix this. I don't know how to tell her this isn't what she thinks it is, and she's got this all wrong. She's not going to believe it, and we'll be stuck right back where we started. This is a fucking helpless place to be in.

"Don't lie to yourself. You've always wanted this. It was always meant to end this way, Reed. You and I both know that." She's got her arms crossed over her chest, putting up a good front, but I can see beyond it. It's killing her to say it as much as it's killing me to hear it.

"No, you're not listening to me," I argue, wanting to take her by the arms and shake her. "This isn't what I want at all, and I'm not sure you understand what I'm saying. This isn't how it started out. I have strong feelings for you." I hope she recognizes the truth in my words, the honesty in my voice. It cracks as I beg her.

"No it's not how it started out," she says. I can see the devastation on her face as she realizes we're not playing parts here anymore. "This is so much more than it started out being. I was dumb to think I could do this," she whispers, real tears coming to her eyes.

"I don't want to let you go."

"That's not what I saw a few minutes ago. I saw you wrapped up in your ex-fiancée. I should have listened to Justin." She laughs, and the sound is bitter. It makes my stomach hurt and my chest cold. "If you wanted me to believe this was real, you have a fucking funny way of showing it. Nothing could have hurt me more than to see her in your arms, and you know that."

"Justin knows nothing about what I feel for you. Fuck, *you* don't know, and you're refusing to listen. I'm ready to talk, please." I'm trying to grasp her hand in mine; trying to hold her to me so she can't leave. I know if she leaves I may not have another chance, and I'm not ready to face that yet. "Listen to what I'm saying to you." I finally grasp her hand and pull it to my chest. My heart is pounding, and the way her pupils dilate, I know she gets it, but she's being fucking stubborn. I'm laying my emotions on the table for both of us to see. It's a gamble, but it's what I have to do.

"All I know is in the end we'll both hurt. This all ends the same way. I don't see us having a future. I can't do that. Not with you. I can't let you take your anger out on me again; I can't let us hate each other when we're done."

I scream at her. I can't help it. I'm so frustrated we're talking in circles. "Because you refuse to listen to reason, Sass. It's changed for both of us. I'm telling you this with my heart on my sleeve."

"It changes until Lacey finally decides she's had enough of the games and you go running back to her. I can't do that," she whispers, the joy I usually hear in her voice gone. Her tone is dead. "Please let me go."

"I will. I'll give you the space you want, but I'm not letting you go permanently. I promise you that. Get used to us, Sass, because we're going to be together for the long haul."

She gives me a look that absolutely breaks my heart. "I wish I could believe you."

"You will. I'll prove it to you." And I know without a doubt I will.

CHAPTER THIRTY

Sass

"YOU'VE GOT TO get out of this office and go on some jobs today," Justin tells me as he sits across from the desk, staring at me like I'm about to break.

It's been two weeks since Reed and I last talked face to face, and to be honest, I'm still raw. There's still a part of me that's been left on the blacktop of my apartment parking lot, and it's getting run over day in and day out. Sure, we text and we talk on the phone, but it's missing something. An innocence we had in the beginning. I haven't gone anywhere since that day besides this office and back home. "I don't know if I can, Justin. I don't know if I'm up for that." I'm fighting depression, and the fact he wants me to brush it off gets me madder than I ever thought it would.

"Look, you can't keep wallowing around in this bullshit. I'm going to tell him the same thing. So what? You took a chance and it backfired, or you think it did. I'm not even sure what the fuck is going on with the two of you right now. I know y'all are still talking. What I don't understand is why you don't work this shit out. You have the option, but you're being too fucking stubborn," he continues. "Either figure it out or move on. Stop texting, stop calling, and stop fucking stringing him on."

"Me? String him on? I did this to help him," I defend my

actions. "My intentions were in the right place."

"You and I both know that's a crock of shit. You did this because you wanted to know what it would be like to be with him. You were purely selfish, and now it's come back to bite you in the ass," Justin argues. "He's offered you what you want, and you're too scared to take a shot when real feelings are on the line. Fine. Do whatever the fuck you want, but stop moping around and stop bringing him with you. He has a life to live just like you do, and I'll be damned if I lose him again the way I lost him before because of some woman."

My mouth hangs open as Justin gives me his back and leaves. The truth is hard to take, but I know he's right. I know I need to make some sort of decision, and I need to make it soon.

MY DAY HAS gone from bad to worse as I sit in line at the gas station with my low fuel light on. I try not to think of the last time this happened. Reed had been in the next stall over, and with a few words, a few glances, and a night at his house, he changed my life.

I know today he won't be there. There won't be any life-changing moments this night. Finally it's my turn, and I pull my car up, popping the gas cap from inside and then climbing out to start the process. I'm not even aware of my surroundings until I've already inserted the nozzle and started filling it up. A female voice from one stall over catches my attention.

"Sass Straight, you look like shit."

I'd know that voice anywhere, and today is not the day for it to make fun of me. I finish pumping my gas and hang the nozzle back up, turning off the pump. As my back is to her, I gather my courage and I square my shoulders. I'm going to say a few things to Lacey.

"You look like a whore, but I keep that to myself every time I see you." I walk over.

There is no way this woman is going to see how distraught I am because Reed and I can't get our shit together. Her eyes narrow at me, and she takes in a breath.

"You don't know me."

I'm over to her now, and our similar height means I don't have to look up or down; I can look straight into her eyes. "Oh, I do. I know your type. You play the damsel in distress whenever you need someone to fix something for you. You string along men and let them pay your way, and then when you're bored with one, you move on to the next."

"At least I don't like sloppy seconds." She gives me a grin that I guess is supposed to be triumphant.

"I've loved Reed since I was a kid, and I would take him any way I can get him. That's not sloppy seconds—that's a lifetime commitment you'll never be able to make." I stare at her until a guy catches my attention, and I realize Taylor is with her. Perfect.

"You want to talk about sloppy seconds? Taylor has been hitting on me since I was thirteen-years old. He always wanted me, but I guess you're second best, and if that's all he can get, that's what he'll take."

Fuck, that felt good. With a smile on my face for the first time in weeks, I walk back over to my car. Turning back towards them, I flash Taylor a smile. "I hope you enjoyed the blowjob you watched, 'cause that's all you'll ever get of me." This has changed absolutely nothing for Reed and me, but I hope it lets me move on. With or without him.

Reed

"I DON'T WANT to run her off," I tell Justin as I help my guys lay drywall. He's come today to listen to me bitch and to help me work. In moments like this, I realize exactly what a friend I have in him. "I feel like she thinks everything I say is a line, and I don't know how to make her believe I'm being honest. I tried honesty, and it blew up in my face. It's not like I don't realize how we started off this relationship, but at some point for both of us, it became real, but she refuses to acknowledge it. I've never met a more infuriating woman in my life."

"I don't know." Justin grabs the other side of the drywall, helping me hold it. "Maybe you should show her with actions, not words. Sass has never been good at listening, even when she was a kid. She was more of an action learner. Maybe she hears what you're saying, but it doesn't mean anything to her because you haven't proven it to her," he says. "I may be completely off base because I'm her older brother and not someone who wants to look at her the way you do, but that's one thing I do know about her. Maybe it could help you."

I roll the idea around in my head. She is a woman of action; she never lets anyone do something for her that she can do for herself. Could that work? What would it hurt if it didn't? It can't be any worse than where we are now. Finally I come to a decision. "You know what? You might be right."

"She's off tomorrow," Justin offers "And I won't be interfering again. I've said my piece to you both."

I can work with that. I just hope she's open to it. And if she's not? Well, tough shit, she's still going to hear me out.

CHAPTER THIRTY-ONE

Sass

THIS IS IT. This is the last day I wallow in my misery. When these twenty-four hours are over, I'll make a damn decision about what I want to do, how I want to live life from now on, and I'll damn well stick with it.

For these twenty-four hours, I'm watching some stupid talk show on TV and eating my weight in these chocolate chip cookies I've made. When my doorbell rings, I jump and then curse. *Shit.* The only person who knows I'm off today is Justin, and I begged him to leave me alone, not to check on me, and to let me get over it. He is who he is though, and I know he always has to make sure I'm okay.

I don't even look through the peephole before opening the door. "Justin, I'm fine."

"That's great, but I'm not Justin."

The voice that greets me is one I've wanted to hear in person for weeks. There have been times I wanted to drive by his house and peek in, just to see his face. When I look up, I'm floored by how he takes my breath away. It's like I forgot how he looked. He's never been more of a welcome sight to me.

Reed stands in front of me, holding a basket. I stare at him, my mouth open for the longest time. Finally, he asks with an amused grin on his face. "Can I come in?"

I step aside, letting him enter my apartment. I look behind him to make sure there are no cameras following, to make sure I'm not getting pranked. When I close the door, I turn to him. "What are you doing here?"

"This is what it's going to take, right? I have to prove to you I'm in this for the long haul? That I'm not playing around? I decided you need to know some truths without anyone eavesdropping on our conversation. I need you to know things when you know no one is watching. Know this, I'm not doing this for anyone's benefit but my own."

My mouth is dry as I watch him. I'm scared of what he has planned, but it's obvious he's gone to some trouble here. "Fine." I have a seat on the couch, trying to act like I don't care.

"This is how well I know you." He grabs the basket and puts it on my coffee table. I'm intrigued as he starts taking things out of it.

"A can of Coke, because you love the cans more than the two-liters or the glass bottles. It's your little treat you give yourself every day." He sets the can of Coke down and grabs a bottle of water. "Smart Water, because you're a water snob and this is the only thing you'll drink out of a bottle or tap. Mounds bars, because you love anything chocolate and coconut. Dirty Dancing, because it's one of your favorite movies. Brantley Gilbert's CD, because you dragged Justin and me to that free concert down on the riverfront. An Alabama Hoodie, because you love football."

I have tears in my eyes as I listen to him name off all my favorite things, laying them out as he empties the basket. I had no idea he knew this much about me, or he even cared this much. It touches me in a way I can't understand, I can't articulate. Finally, he gets to the last thing in the box, and he stops for a minute, taking a deep breath. He holds out a key to me. My eyes are locked on the object he holds as he extends it with a shaking hand.

"A key to my house. I want you to be able to be with me any time you want to be. I want you to be comfortable with me." He takes a shaky breath. "And I love you enough to give this a try again."

A cry escapes my throat as I throw myself at him, tears streaming down my face. He's laid himself bare before me in a way I never thought he would. This is more than I ever expected from him, more than I could have dreamed of. I grab the key, sniffing, realizing what this means, realizing this is everything I've ever wanted.

"I love you too."

"Then please, don't make me wait anymore," he pleads. "Let's stop hurting each other, stop being miserable, and get on with our lives."

I throw myself at him, melting in his arms. His mouth catches mine, and he kisses me with a passion I've never let myself experience with anyone but him. I'm the happiest I've ever been in this place. His arms are the only place I want to be—ever again.

CHAPTER THIRTY-TWO

Sass

I GIGGLE AS I sit at the table with Reed and our friends at Hank's. Morgan and I are looking over a wedding magazine—she and Justin have finally set a date, and now she desperately wants to have everything done yesterday. The drinks we've had are making the job hilarious.

"This will be your perfect maid-of-honor dress." She points to a horrendous orange number.

"Orange is definitely not my color. If that's what you want me to wear, I'm gonna move Reed out of the best man position and wear a tux."

Hearing his name, Reed slings his arm around my shoulder and pulls me close. His mouth on my ear, he talks loudly so I can hear him over the music and the crowd. "I'm sure you'd make a tux look like a million bucks."

I blush and lean my body into his. This is the kind of mush he's turned me into over the past few months. There is no way I can truly express my sorrow for it, but the old me sometimes scolds the new me for being putty in his hands. Then, I look at Justin and Morgan. They're paired off too, and he's actively looking through the magazine, showing her what he thinks would look good on her. I have to remind myself this is our new lives. Things are easier and simpler now.

"I bet you say that to all the women," I tease.

He cups my jaw with his hand and brings my face down to his for a kiss. "Only the ones I want to spend the rest of my life with."

My breath stops for almost a full beat. This isn't the first time he's said something like that to me, and I wonder when he's going to make it official, because I'm ready. Like fifteen years ready, but I know by the look in his eyes he's cautious.

That's okay, I can be cautious too, and I can be patient.

"I'm here whenever you want to do that." I lean into his throat and place a kiss there against the strong pulse.

"One day, Sass, and I don't think it's going to be very long from now, but I want to make sure it's right. I want to make sure there's nothing hanging over us, and nobody in the background who's gonna try to sabotage us. I want to make sure it's perfect for us."

I nod, because I understand. I know where he's coming from; nobody wants to mess up an engagement twice. I offer him a saucy smile. "I'll be right here waiting for you when you're ready. In the meantime, let's give these lovebirds some space and hit the dance floor. I want everyone here to know what kind of moves my man has."

I know he likes when I call him mine. The words do exactly what I want them to do. He stands, grabs my hand, puffs out his chest, and pulls me to the dance floor.

Reed

I TWIRL SASS around the dance floor, holding her close as a slower song comes on the jukebox. In the past six months we've figured things out; things still aren't perfect, but we're making it work. We make compromises for each other. I'm not the one expected to drop everything and come home to her, and she's not expected to do the same with me. As two small business owners, it's not easy, but it's worth it.

"Thanks for coming out tonight." Her nails dig into my long-sleeve shirt. "It's been a while since we've had time."

I tilt her head back, looking into her eyes as I tower over her. "You know I'll always make time for you, baby."

And I do, it's my number-one priority. The two of us stay busy, helping each of the businesses we're involved in, but our relationship takes a front seat. It's nice to have someone who understands when I have to make the hard decisions for the bottom line of the business. She gets it when I'm stuck at work because two of my crew have sick kids and there's a deadline on a project. There's no judgment, and to me that's the best part of all. I'm free to do what I need to do, as long as we make time for each other.

Making time is easier now. Just two weeks ago she moved into my house permanently, and I danced a little jig that day. What was once my and Lacey's house, is now my and Sass' home. She's made it that way with little touches that are hers, with the way she welcomes my friends. Every Saturday, we have dinner for everybody. She plans it, and I love to see her walk around the kitchen like she owns it. She's given herself permission to be my partner in life, and I've never been happier. Most days I can't even wipe the smile off my face.

She's a fixture in my life for however long I'm blessed to be here, and I can't wait to make it happen, but I know it's something I'll never rush again. When it happens this time, it'll be right, and there won't be a long engagement. I don't want this woman to get away from me. She makes my life whole and makes no apologies for it. This is the type of love you don't ever give up. I've learned the lesson loud and clear.

"You almost ready to get out of here?" I ask her, letting my hand slide slightly up the back of her sweater. It's a soft touch, and one I give without reservation now.

I'm still unable to get enough of her. I don't think I'll ever be able to. She leans into me, rubbing up against my chest. "I'm ready whenever you are."

Turning her towards the table we're sitting at with our friends, I let her go and encourage her to walk. "Then let's move this someplace more private."

She shoots me a glance and a smile. It's her naughty smile, and my jeans tighten as I realize I'm probably about to get lucky in the parking lot. Which we all know wouldn't be the first time.

We get to our table, make our excuses, and say goodbye to our friends. As we pass the other tables to get to the door, we pass Lacey and Taylor. The need to thank both of them has been growing over the past few months, but I can't seem to make myself do it. Thanking them doesn't necessarily seem like a douche move, but it's been quiet with them, and I don't want to cause trouble where there isn't any right now. If they knew what they'd done in the end, they would be so pissed at themselves. Instead of ruining my life, they made it better. Because if it hadn't been for his dick in her mouth, I would have never gotten a little Sass in mine.

The End

If you liked Sass…you'll *love Sketch!*

Blurb

My name is Devin, but everybody calls me Sketch. I opened my own tattoo shop two years ago, and I've finally gotten to the point where I'm going to be able to give my wife everything she's ever wanted. I'm going to be able to take time off and spend a day a week with her. In fact, tonight, I stopped and grabbed some wine, got her flowers, and those chocolates she likes.

What I wasn't prepared for was to be met at the front door by her carrying her shit out.

She loves me, but she's not in love with me anymore. What kind of bullshit excuse is that? *I've left her alone too often, I've been completely focused on one goal, and apparently she's sick of waiting.*

So here I stand. Half the man I was, pissed as fuck, because while I was busy making a better life for us, she was under the impression I was leaving her lonely. I know one day she'll see what I've been doing has been for us, and when that day comes… *She* can damn well come crawling back to *me*.

Prologue

Sketch

"**I** LOVE YOU, but I'm no longer *in love* with you, Devin."

The words echo off the hardwood floor I had paid to have put in our home, they bounce off the walls Nina and I had painstakingly painted yellow. I remember the argument we got into about the trim color; an argument I won by tackling her to the, then carpeted, floor and fucking her into submission. *What had happened to that couple? When had that changed?*

"I don't even know what to say." And I didn't. Shock and something akin to anger boil in my gut. I want to scream and punch, ask what the fuck is wrong with her, but those words won't come. I can't push them past my lips.

She sighs. "That's precisely the problem, Devin; you never know what to say. You never know when you're going to be home, you never know what your schedule is going to be. I can't do this. When was the last time we had sex? When was the last time *you* told *me* that you love me? Devin, I'm done."

There it is again. My real name. For the past seven years I've been Sketch. Through my apprenticeship and now at my own shop. Most people don't even know my real fuckin' name, and here she's used it twice in one conversation.

"You're done?" I sound like a parrot, but I can't help it. This shit is coming out of left field for me. I'm standing here like a

160

chump, holding a bouquet of flowers, a bottle of wine, and a box of chocolates. Following her out to the driveway, I watch as she walks awkwardly, holding duffel bags in each arm.

"Yeah, Devin. Done." She rolls her eyes and continues putting her stuff in the car. The car, I might add, I bought her with the first profit that my shop turned.

"Do you even see what I'm holding, Nina?" I ask, thrusting my hands towards her.

"It's too late," she tells me, finally showing some emotion.

There are tears in her eyes and I wonder why. It's not like I'm the one leaving her. I still have no idea where any of this is coming from. "Too late? This is me telling you that I finally have the time. Babe, we're gonna live our lives."

"I've *been* living, Devin." She stomps her foot. "It's you who's had your head up your ass at that goddamn tattoo shop."

That's it. My stomach drops, and I see for the first time the ungrateful bitch she's become. I feel anger overtake me. "That goddamn tattoo shop has provided you with a good life, Nina," I yell.

Throwing the stuff down I have in my hands, I let it smash into a million pieces and watch it roll towards the car. Just like my life, it's a jumbled up mess of shattered hopes and a river full of broken dreams.

Coming in 2017!

Renegade

(subject to change)

Prologue

Whitney

"RYAN, I'M TELLIN' you. I need my hair pulled, I need my ass smacked, I need someone paying attention to my nipples, a dick in my treasure cove. I need it all."

Drunk. I am drunk. Like way past the legal limit – otherwise I wouldn't be sitting here spilling all of my secrets to my baby brother's best friend. The baby brother that had been totally unplanned by my parents. Ten years my junior, baby brother. He and Ryan are the same age; twenty-five to my thirty-five.

I see him try to suppress a grin as he brings his bottle of beer up to his lips, taking a nice long pull off of it. I am mesmerized by the way his throat muscles move when he swallows. "How many of those have you had to drink?"

His voice is as smooth as the wine I swirl in my glass. I tilt my head to the side, realizing that the whole room tilts too. Counting back, I try to think how many I had before he took the seat next to mine, and I can't remember. "Five or six?" I ask him, like he should know.

"You think maybe it's time you quit for the night?" He asks.

"Quit?" I ask, and run my tongue over my dry lips, trying to make them so that they can speak easier. "Quitting is not something I do. That's what my ex-husband did. My mama did. That's what my former boss did," I shake my head, and try to stand up on four-inch stilettos. He reaches out and grabs my elbow, steadying me. "Whitney Trumbolt is not a fuckin' quitter."

I can see Ryan try again to keep the smile from his face. The corners of his lips twitch, and it pisses me off.

"You think this is funny?" I take another drink from my wine glass. It's a big one this time, I drain it down.

"No, Whit, I think you're having a bad night."

A bad night? Try a bad decade. If I could do anything, it would go back to the night I turned twenty-five, and be the age that Ryan is again. I would do so many things different, I would change so much about the choices that I made back then. "You know nothing about me, other than the fact that I'm Tank's sister."

He grabs me by the wrist, locking his fingers around the skin and bone. I never realized until this moment how much bigger he is than me. Never really paid any kind of attention to it – oh I've paid attention to him off and on through-out the years, but never like this.

Ryan "Renegade" Kepler rises to his full height, towering over me as I do my best to keep my footing and ignore the way my skin tingles where he is gripping my wrist. He leans in close – so close I can feel his breath on my skin.

"I know a lot of things about you that you don't think I know."

His voice is hard and soft at the same time. I close my eyes to savor it. This is the closest I've been to a man in a *very* long time.

"I know that you love your mama's fried chicken, your grandmother's homemade mac and cheese, Alabama football, and Dale Earnhardt Jr. I know that you have a soft heart. Hallmark movies make you cry, you pick up strays on the side of the road, and you always buy that homeless man over on near the Starbucks a morning coffee," he tells me.

I'm wrapped up in his voice, in the things he *does* know about me. Things I never knew that he'd paid attention to. I'm swaying, but it's because his voice is doing weird things to my equilibrium. His other hand wraps around my hip and I can feel the heat of his body through the material of my skirt.

"I know that your ex-husband was a piece of shit. I know that your ex-boss didn't know what the hell to do with the creative genius that is your mind, and I know that your mama will never forgive you for giving up pageants, but she'll never forgive herself for pushing you that damn hard," he stops and pulls back.

Our eyes meet and I realize with clarity that I'm breathing hard, hard enough that it feels as if I've run a marathon.

"You wanna know what else I know?" he asks.

I'm captivated by the way the dim lights of the bar make his brown eyes seem darker, I'm enthralled by the fact that it looks like it's been a few days since he shaved, and I'm even more fascinated by the cut he has on his cheek. He and Tank went out on a call last night, and I can't help but wonder if that cut is the result of it. I shake my head and then nod, because I do want to find out what else he knows. I step forward, put my arms around his neck, and lean up so that now I'm the one in his ear. "Tell me what else you know."

I see him look around the bar, checking to make sure that

we're not being paid any attention to. He bends with his knees and grips my ass cheeks in his hands. "I know I'm the one that can put my dick in that treasure cove. I know I'm the one that can pull that hair, I can pull on those nipples, and I can smack that ass. The question is – will you let me?"

It's not a question I can say no to. The way the air cackles between us, and the alcohol I've consumed. There's not any way that I can say no.

"Yes," I breath out….adding on a "please."

"Oh baby, you don't have to ask. I'll do whatever you need me to," Ryan says as I find my hand in his and stumble to keep up as he pulls us out of the bar.

In mere minutes I'm in his truck, and we're headed towards his house. I will myself not to pass out, because for the first time in years, I want to be here and present for this experience that's about to happen. I want to remember every damn detail. If it's only going to be for this one night, I don't want to miss a thing.

Note from Laramie

Thank you for purchasing *Sass*! An older brother's best friend romance is something I've wanted to write for a long time. It's one of the types of books I cut my teeth on when I first started reading Romance novels as a teenager.

Thank you for allowing me to do it, and I hope you've enjoyed Reed and Sass' story!

— Laramie

About Laramie

Laramie Briscoe is the best-selling author of the Heaven Hill Series & the Rockin' Country Series.

Since self-publishing her first book in May of 2013, Laramie Briscoe has published over 10 books. She's appeared on the Top 100 Bestselling E-books Lists on iBooks, Amazon Kindle, Kobo, and Barnes & Noble. She's been called "a very young Maya Banks" (Amazon reviewer) and her books have been accused of being "sexy, family-oriented, romances with heart".

When she's not writing alpha males who seriously love their women, she loves spending time with friends, reading, and marathoning shows on her DVR. Married to her high school sweetheart, Laramie lives in Bowling Green, KY with her husband (the Travel Coordinator) and a sometimes crazy cat named Beau.

Connect with Laramie

Email:

laramie.briscoe@gmail.com

Website:

www.laramiebriscoe.com

Facebook:

facebook.com/AuthorLaramieBriscoe

Twitter:

twitter.com/LaramieBriscoe

Pinterest:

pinterest.com/laramiebriscoe

Instagram:

instagram.com/laramie_briscoe

Substance B:

substance-b.com/LaramieBriscoe.html

Mailing List:

eepurl.com/Fi4N9

32309555R00111

Made in the USA
Middletown, DE
30 May 2016